#12 "Tinker Bell and the Lost Treasure"

Contents

PAPERCUTZ

NEW YORK

"The Scepter"
Concept and Script: Augusto Macchetto
Revised Captions: Cortney Faye Powell
Layout: Denise Shimabukuro
Pencils: Manuela Razzi
Inks: Roberta Zanotta
Color: Studio Kawaii
Letters: Janice Chiang
Page 5 art:
Concept: Tea Orsi
Pencils and Inks: Sara Storino
Color: Andrea Cagol

"The Magical Mirror of Incanta"
Concept and Script: Augusto Macchetto
Revised Captions: Cortney Faye Powell
Layout: Denise Shimabukuro
Pencils: Manuela Razzi
Inks: Roberta Zanotta
Color: Studio Kawaii
Letters: Janice Chiang
Page 31 Art:
Concept: Tea Orsi
Pencils and Inks: Sara Storino
Color: Andrea Cagol

"Towards the Island"
Concept and Script: Augusto Macchetto
Revised Captions: Cortney Faye Powell
Layout: Denise Shimabukuro
Pencils: Manuela Razzi
Inks: Marina Baggio
Color: Studio Kawaii
Letters: Janice Chiang
Page 18 Art:
Concept: Tea Orsi
Pencils and Inks: Sara Storino
Color: Andrea Cagol

"The Glow of Friendship"
Concept and Script: Augusto Macchetto
Revised Captions: Cortney Faye Powell
Layout: Denise Shimabukuro
Pencils: Manuela Razzi
Inks: Roberta Zanotta
Color: Studio Kawaii
Letters: Janice Chiang
Page 44 Art:
Concept: Tea Orsi
Pencils and Inks: Sara Storino
Color: Andrea Cagol

Production – Dawn K. Guzzo
Special Thanks – John Tanzer and Shiho Tilley
Production Coordinator – Beth Scorzato
Associate Editor – Michael Petranek
Jim Salicrup
Editor-in-Chief

ISBN: 978-1-59707-428-5 paperback edition
ISBN: 978-1-59707-429-2 hardcover edition

Printed in China
April 2013 by Asia One Printing LTD
13/F Asia One Tower
8 Fung Yip St., Chaiwan
Hong Kong

Papercutz books may be purchased for business or promotional use.
For information on bulk purchases please contact
Macmillan Corporate and Premium Sales Department at
(800) 221-7945 x5442.

Distributed by Macmillan
First Papercutz Printing

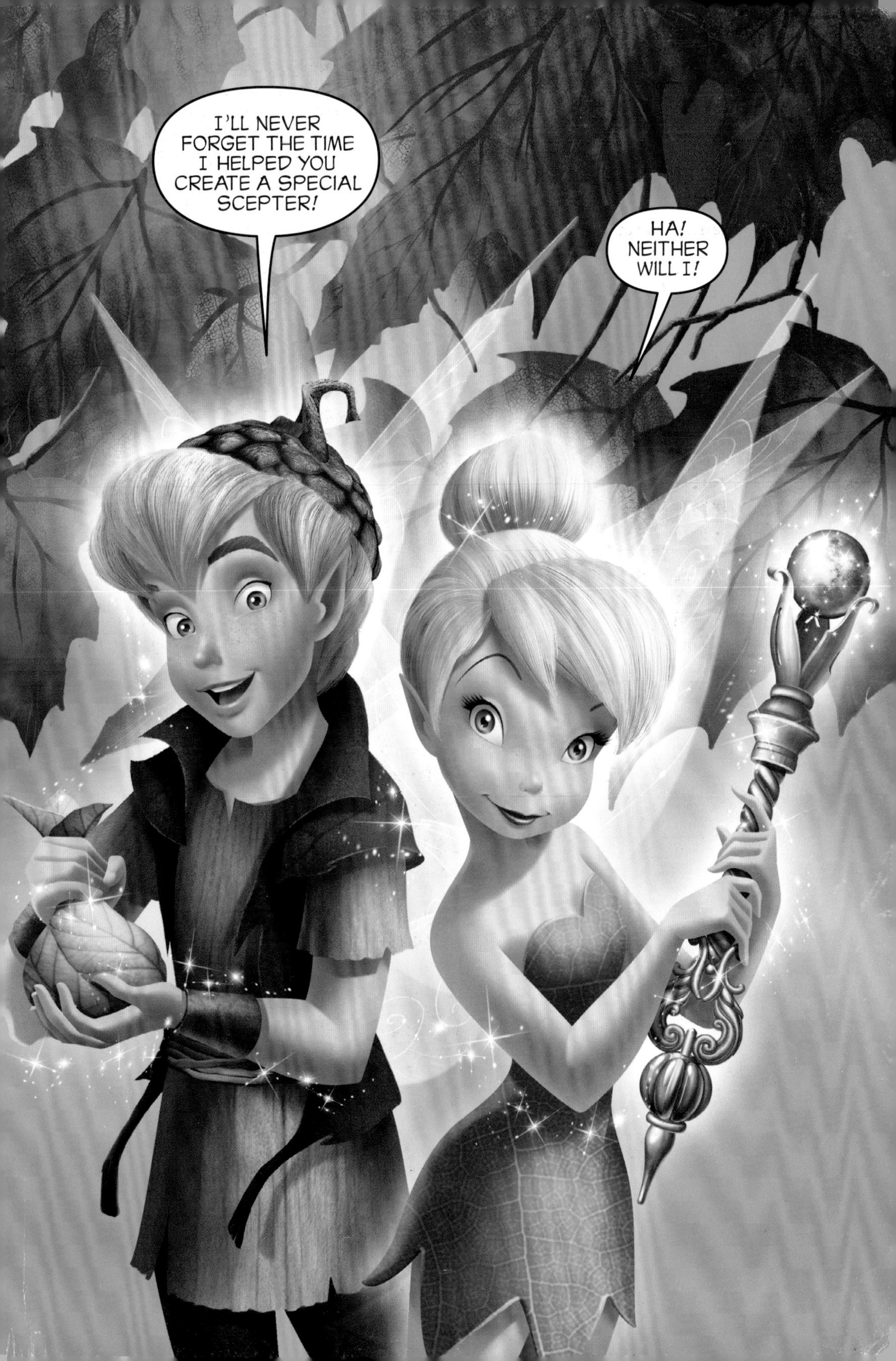
I'LL NEVER FORGET THE TIME I HELPED YOU CREATE A SPECIAL SCEPTER!
HA! NEITHER WILL I!

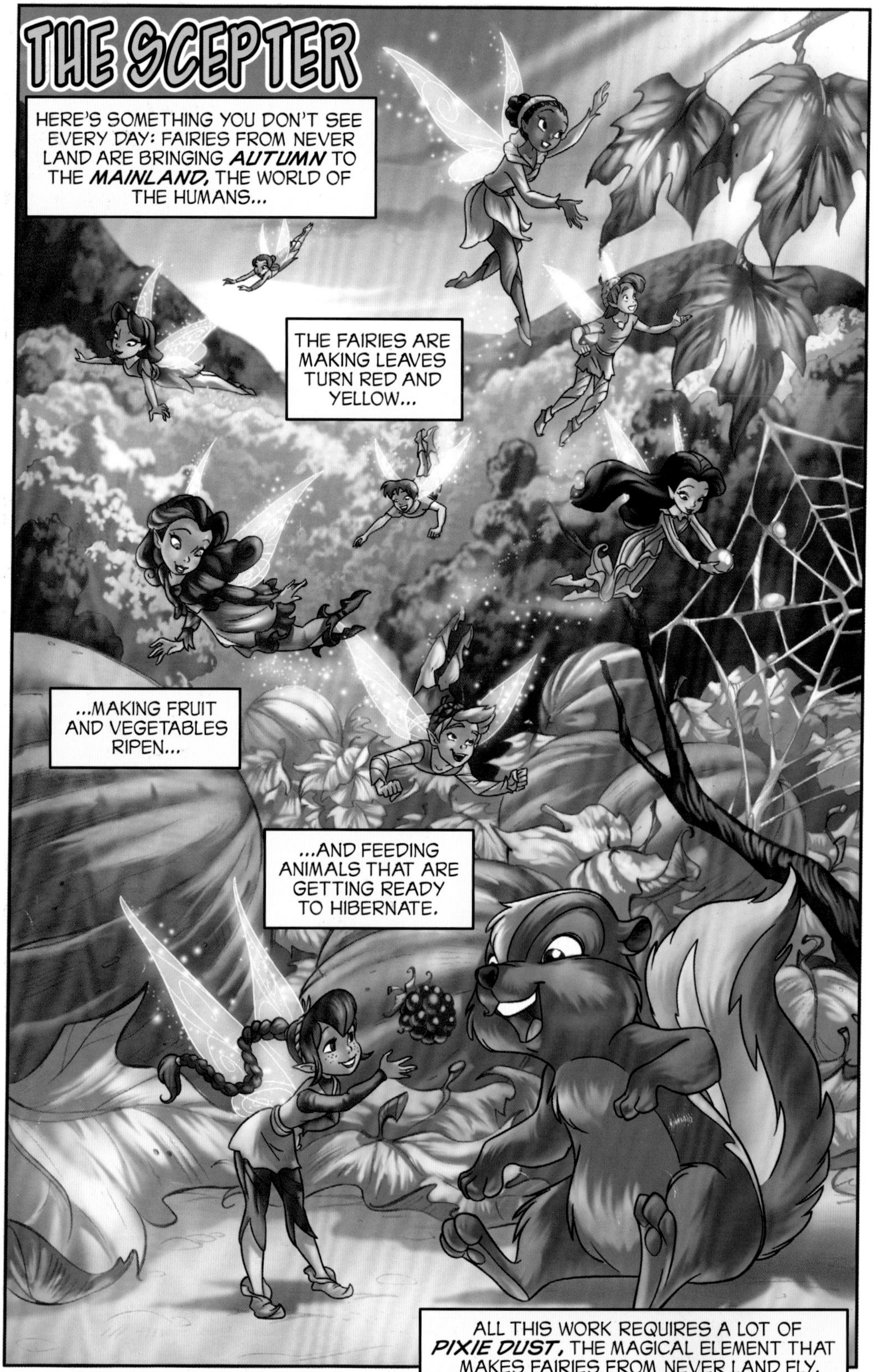
THE SCEPTER
HERE'S SOMETHING YOU DON'T SEE EVERY DAY: FAIRIES FROM NEVER LAND ARE BRINGING AUTUMN TO THE MAINLAND, THE WORLD OF THE HUMANS...
THE FAIRIES ARE MAKING LEAVES TURN RED AND YELLOW...
...MAKING FRUIT AND VEGETABLES RIPEN...
...AND FEEDING ANIMALS THAT ARE GETTING READY TO HIBERNATE.
ALL THIS WORK REQUIRES A LOT OF PIXIE DUST, THE MAGICAL ELEMENT THAT MAKES FAIRIES FROM NEVER LAND FLY.

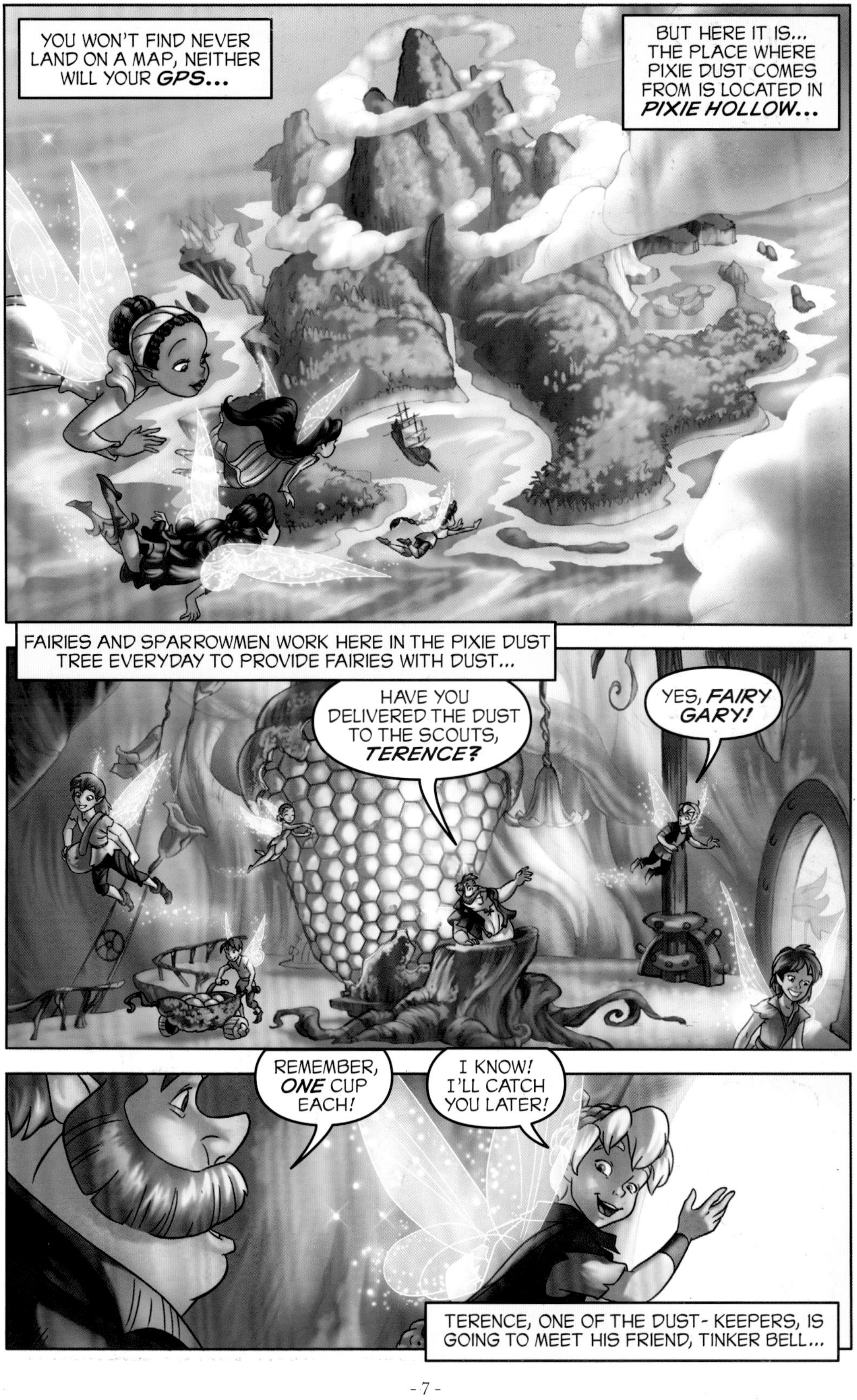
YOU WON'T FIND NEVER LAND ON A MAP, NEITHER WILL YOUR GPS...
BUT HERE IT IS... THE PLACE WHERE PIXIE DUST COMES FROM IS LOCATED IN PIXIE HOLLOW...
FAIRIES AND SPARROWMEN WORK HERE IN THE PIXIE DUST TREE EVERYDAY TO PROVIDE FAIRIES WITH DUST...
HAVE YOU DELIVERED THE DUST TO THE SCOUTS, TERENCE?
YES, FAIRY GARY!
REMEMBER, ONE CUP EACH!
I KNOW! I'LL CATCH YOU LATER!
TERENCE, ONE OF THE DUST- KEEPERS, IS GOING TO MEET HIS FRIEND, TINKER BELL...

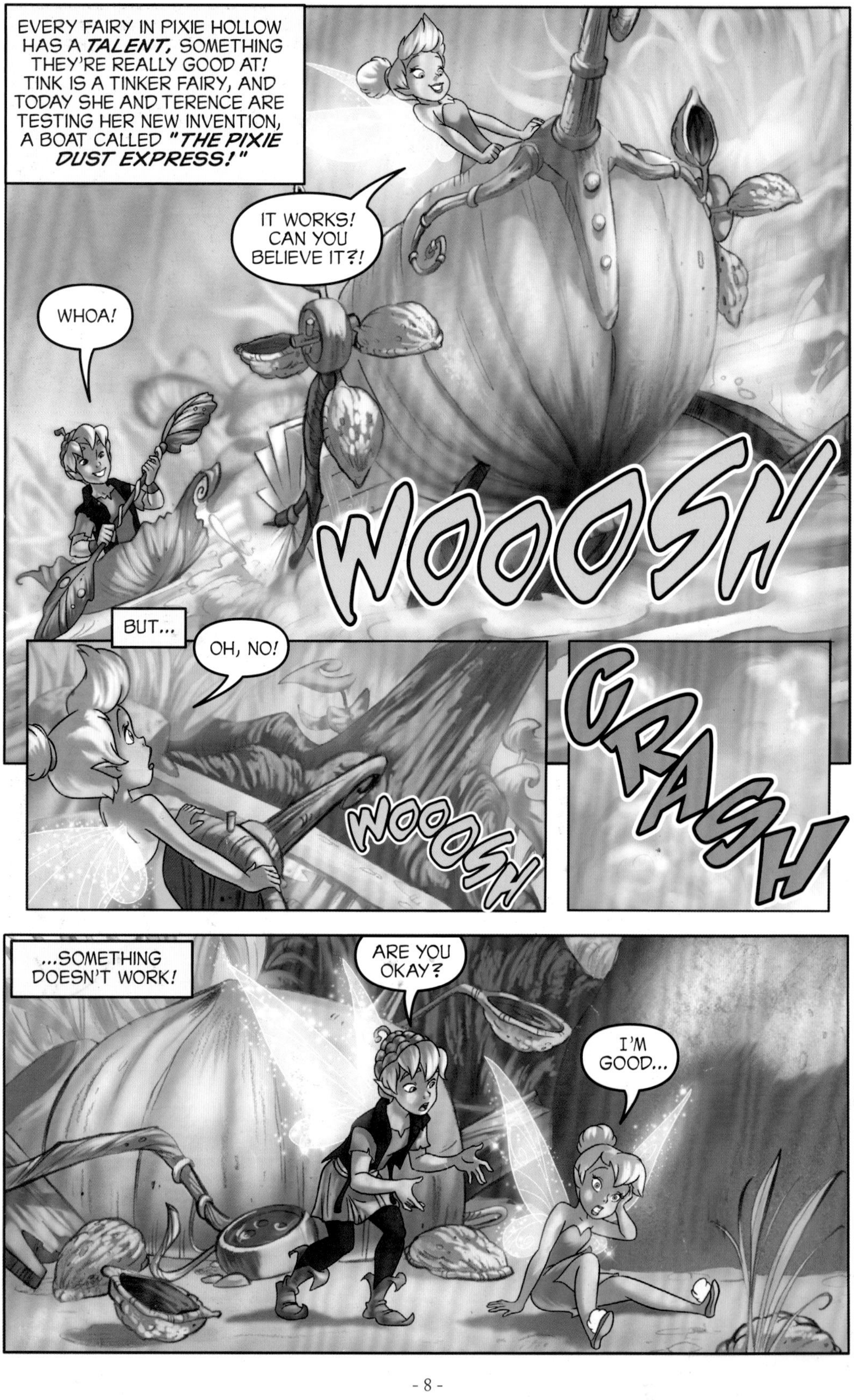
EVERY FAIRY IN PIXIE HOLLOW HAS A *TALENT,* SOMETHING THEY'RE REALLY GOOD AT! TINK IS A TINKER FAIRY, AND TODAY SHE AND TERENCE ARE TESTING HER NEW INVENTION, A BOAT CALLED *"THE PIXIE DUST EXPRESS!"*
IT WORKS! CAN YOU BELIEVE IT?!
WHOA!
WOOOSH
BUT...
OH, NO!
WOOOSH
CRASH
...SOMETHING DOESN'T WORK!
ARE YOU OKAY?
I'M GOOD...

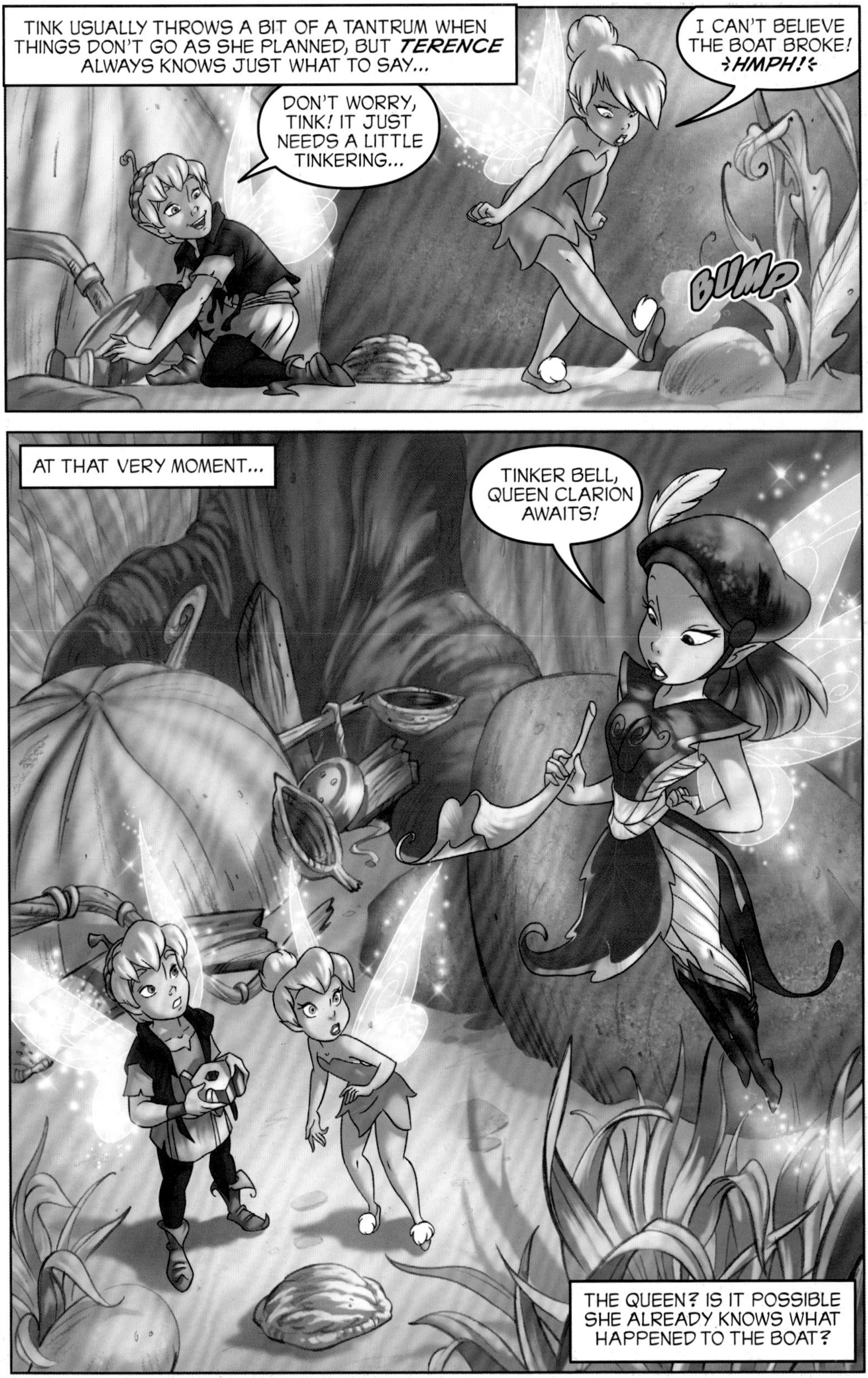
TINK USUALLY THROWS A BIT OF A TANTRUM WHEN THINGS DON'T GO AS SHE PLANNED, BUT *TERENCE* ALWAYS KNOWS JUST WHAT TO SAY...
DON'T WORRY, TINK! IT JUST NEEDS A LITTLE TINKERING...
I CAN'T BELIEVE THE BOAT BROKE! *HMPH!*
BUMP
AT THAT VERY MOMENT...
TINKER BELL, QUEEN CLARION AWAITS!
THE QUEEN? IS IT POSSIBLE SHE ALREADY KNOWS WHAT HAPPENED TO THE BOAT?

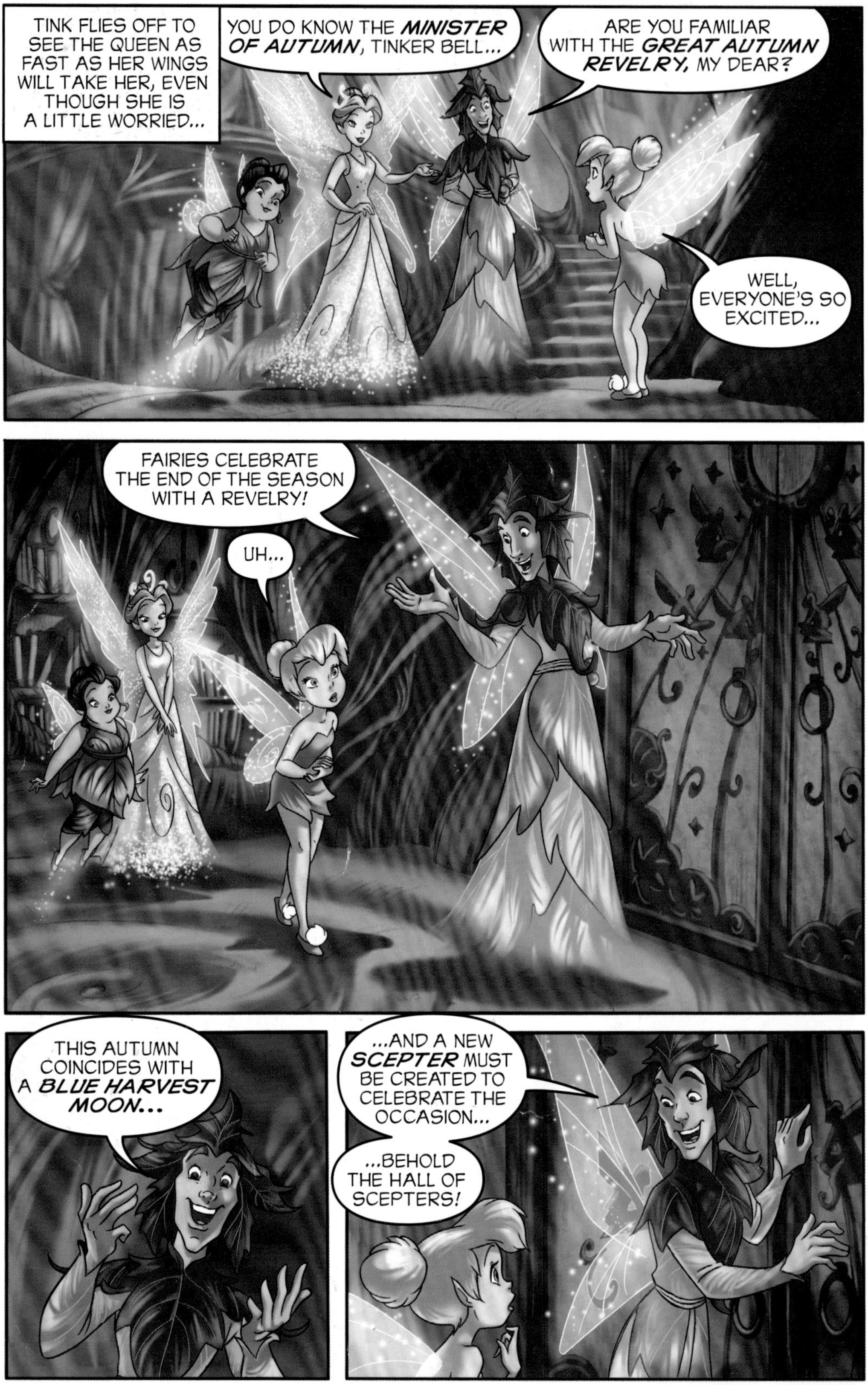
TINK FLIES OFF TO SEE THE QUEEN AS FAST AS HER WINGS WILL TAKE HER, EVEN THOUGH SHE IS A LITTLE WORRIED...
YOU DO KNOW THE *MINISTER OF AUTUMN*, TINKER BELL...
ARE YOU FAMILIAR WITH THE *GREAT AUTUMN REVELRY,* MY DEAR?
WELL, EVERYONE'S SO EXCITED...
FAIRIES CELEBRATE THE END OF THE SEASON WITH A REVELRY!
UH...
THIS AUTUMN COINCIDES WITH A *BLUE HARVEST MOON...*
...AND A NEW *SCEPTER* MUST BE CREATED TO CELEBRATE THE OCCASION...
...BEHOLD THE HALL OF SCEPTERS!

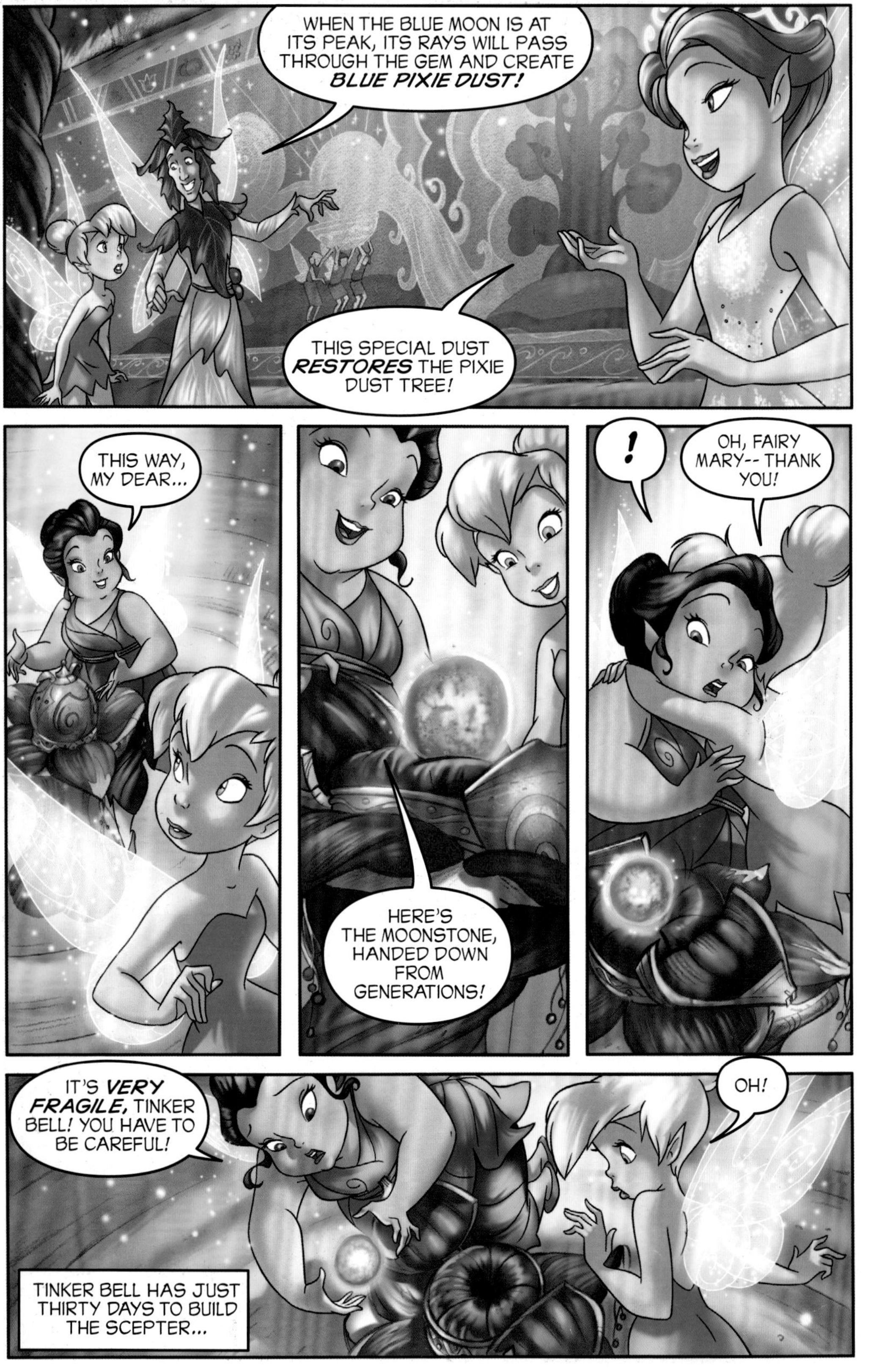
WHEN THE BLUE MOON IS AT ITS PEAK, ITS RAYS WILL PASS THROUGH THE GEM AND CREATE ***BLUE PIXIE DUST!***
THIS SPECIAL DUST ***RESTORES*** THE PIXIE DUST TREE!
THIS WAY, MY DEAR...
HERE'S THE MOONSTONE, HANDED DOWN FROM GENERATIONS!
!
OH, FAIRY MARY-- THANK YOU!
IT'S ***VERY FRAGILE,*** TINKER BELL! YOU HAVE TO BE CAREFUL!
OH!
TINKER BELL HAS JUST THIRTY DAYS TO BUILD THE SCEPTER...

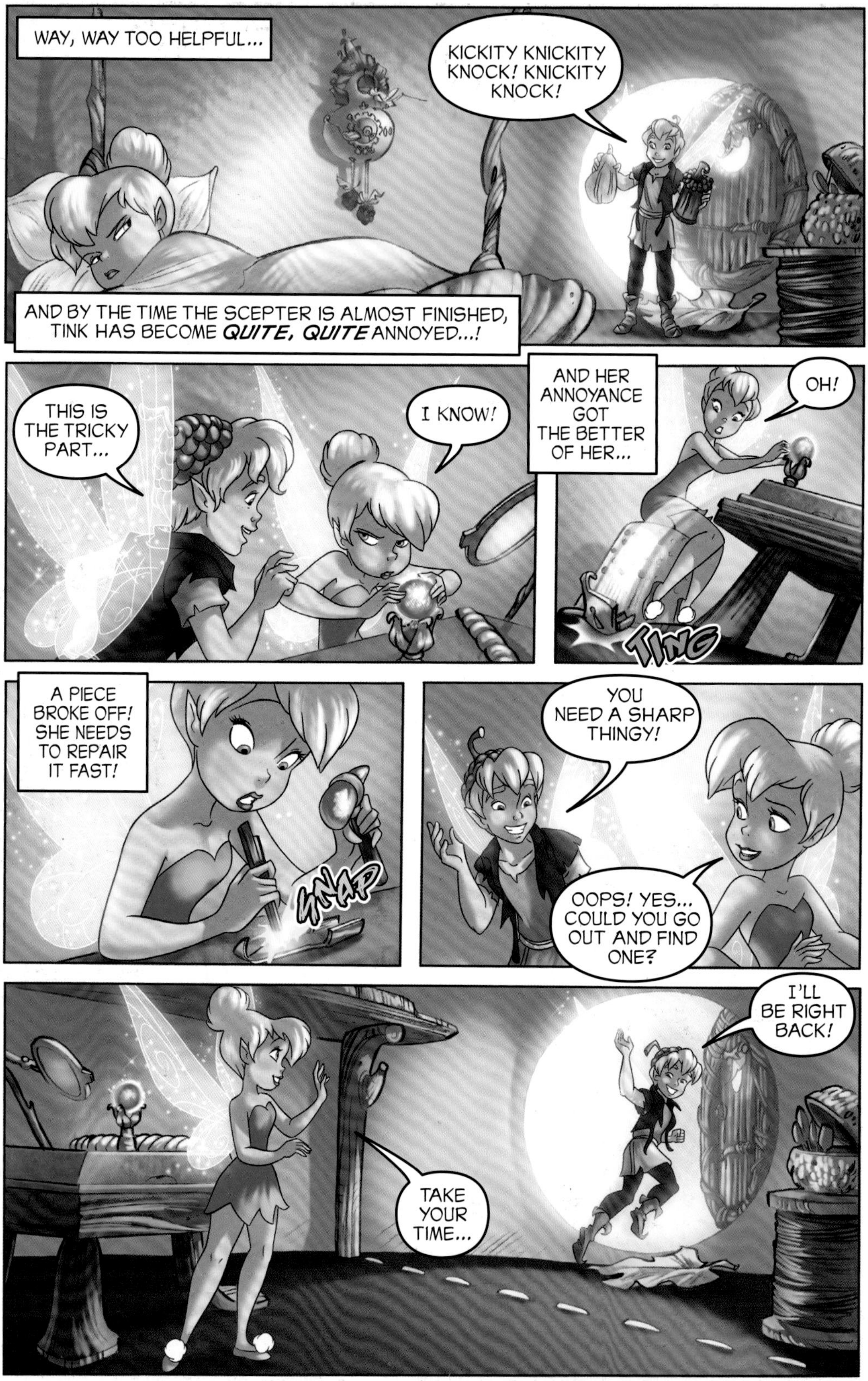
WAY, WAY TOO HELPFUL...
KICKITY KNICKITY KNOCK! KNICKITY KNOCK!
AND BY THE TIME THE SCEPTER IS ALMOST FINISHED, TINK HAS BECOME QUITE, QUITE ANNOYED...!
THIS IS THE TRICKY PART...
I KNOW!
AND HER ANNOYANCE GOT THE BETTER OF HER...
OH!
TING
A PIECE BROKE OFF! SHE NEEDS TO REPAIR IT FAST!
SNAP
YOU NEED A SHARP THINGY!
OOPS! YES... COULD YOU GO OUT AND FIND ONE?
I'LL BE RIGHT BACK!
TAKE YOUR TIME...

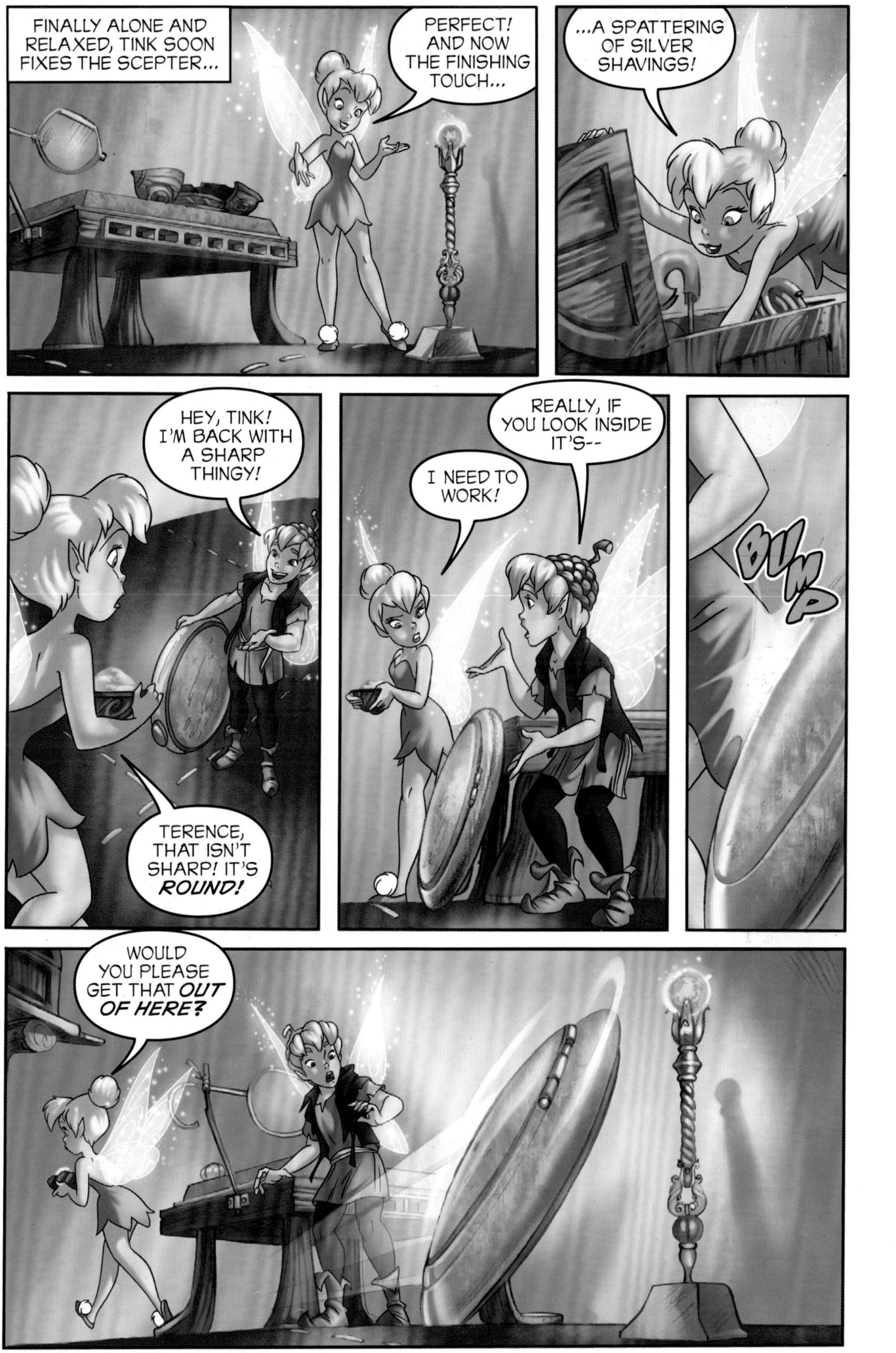
FINALLY ALONE AND RELAXED, TINK SOON FIXES THE SCEPTER...
PERFECT! AND NOW THE FINISHING TOUCH...
...A SPATTERING OF SILVER SHAVINGS!
HEY, TINK! I'M BACK WITH A SHARP THINGY!
TERENCE, THAT ISN'T SHARP! IT'S ROUND!
REALLY, IF YOU LOOK INSIDE IT'S--
I NEED TO WORK!
BUMP
WOULD YOU PLEASE GET THAT OUT OF HERE?

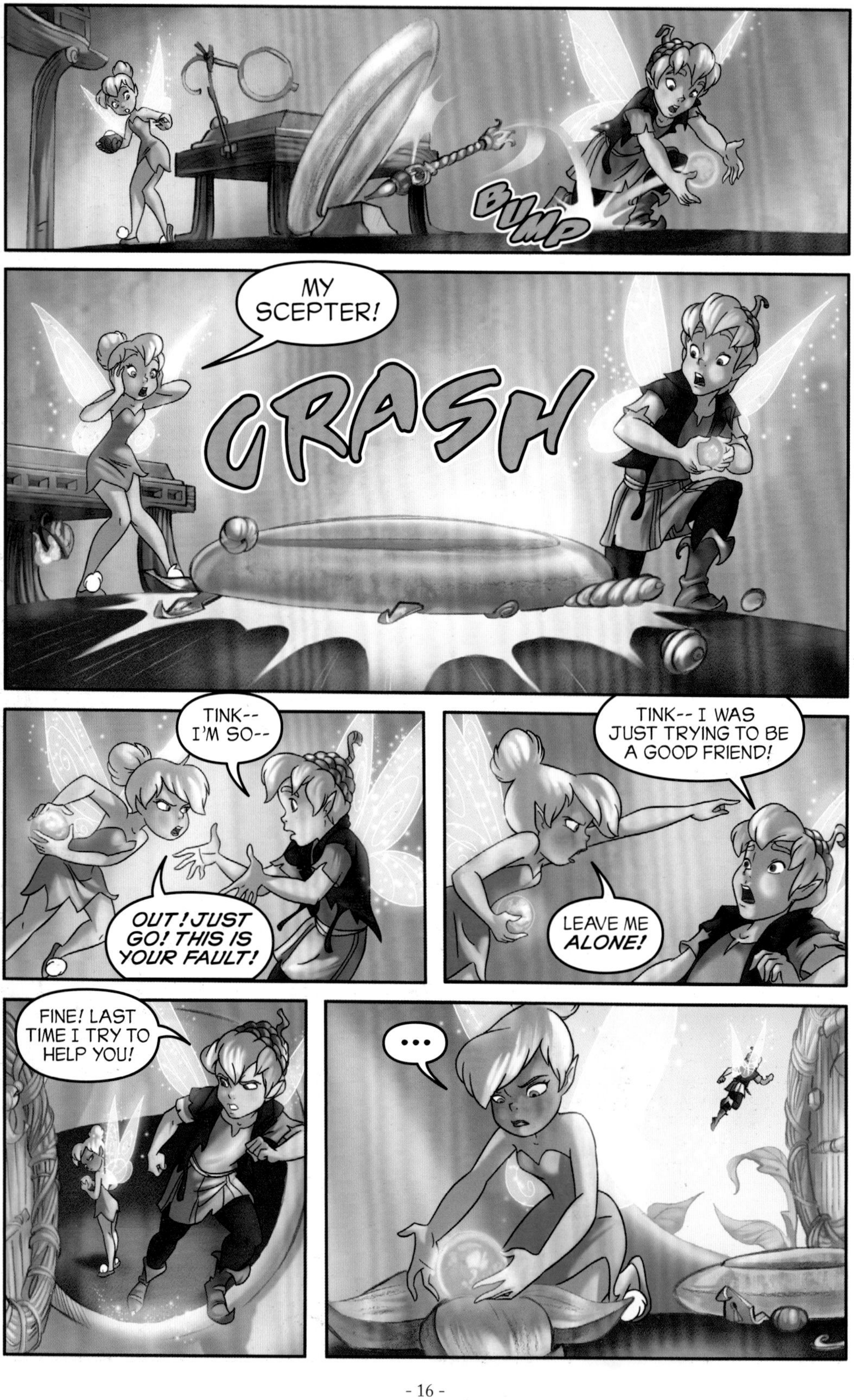
BUMP
MY SCEPTER!
CRASH
TINK-- I'M SO--
OUT! JUST GO! THIS IS YOUR FAULT!
TINK-- I WAS JUST TRYING TO BE A GOOD FRIEND!
LEAVE ME ALONE!
FINE! LAST TIME I TRY TO HELP YOU!
...

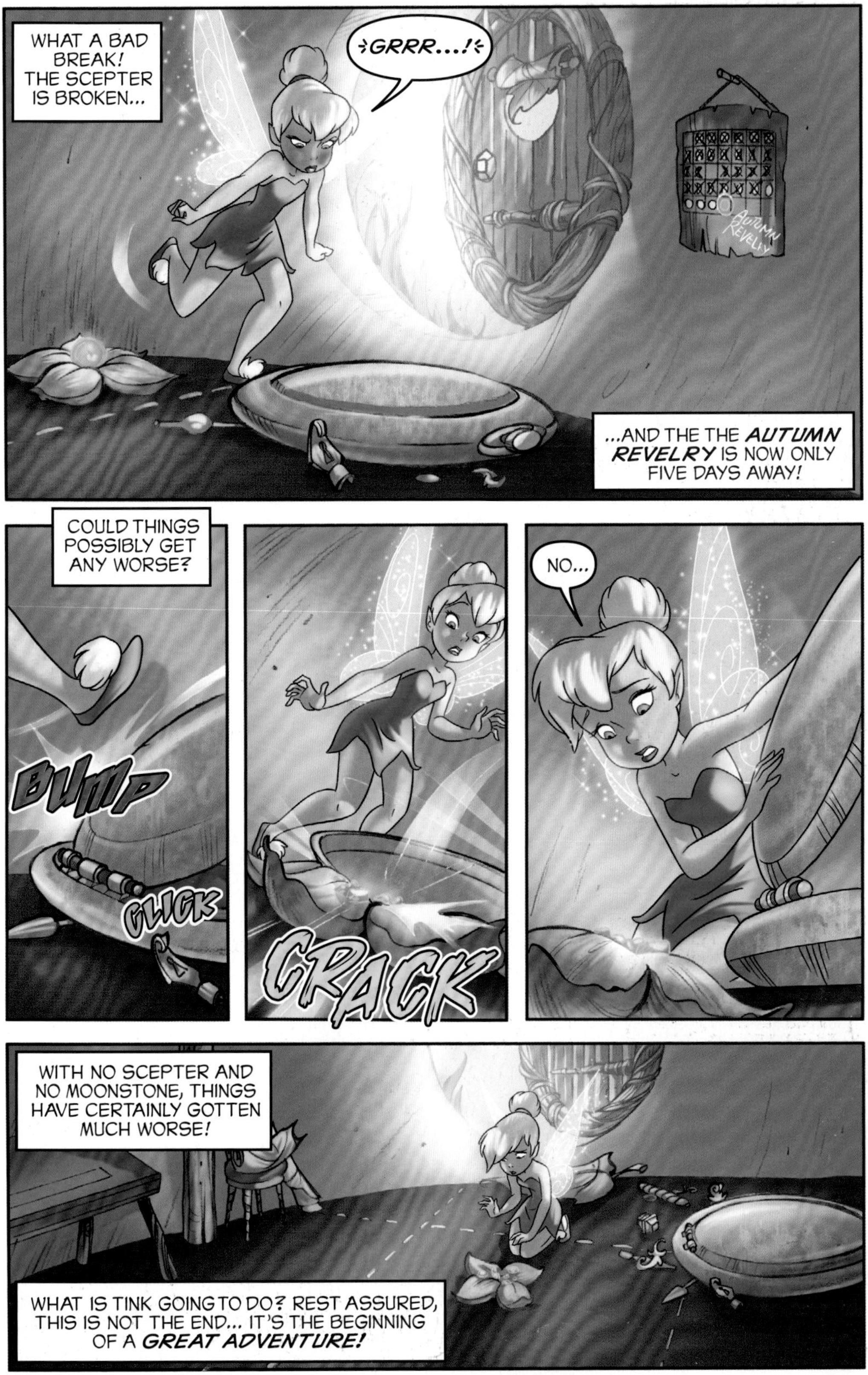

WHAT A BAD BREAK! THE SCEPTER IS BROKEN...
GRRR...!
AUTUMN REVELRY
...AND THE THE AUTUMN REVELRY IS NOW ONLY FIVE DAYS AWAY!
COULD THINGS POSSIBLY GET ANY WORSE?
BUMP
CLICK
CRACK
NO...
WITH NO SCEPTER AND NO MOONSTONE, THINGS HAVE CERTAINLY GOTTEN MUCH WORSE!
WHAT IS TINK GOING TO DO? REST ASSURED, THIS IS NOT THE END... IT'S THE BEGINNING OF A GREAT ADVENTURE!

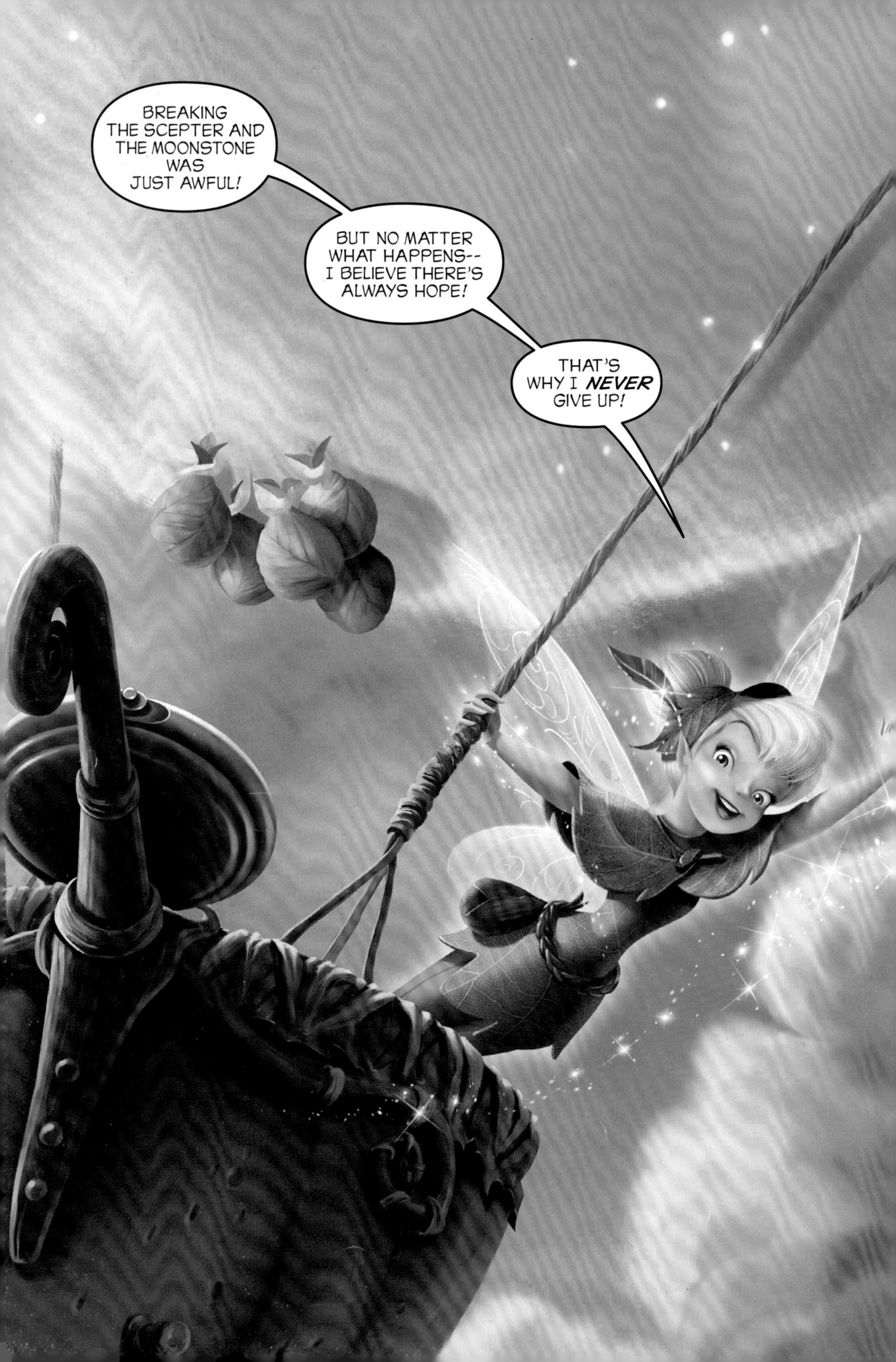
BREAKING THE SCEPTER AND THE MOONSTONE WAS JUST AWFUL!
BUT NO MATTER WHAT HAPPENS-- I BELIEVE THERE'S ALWAYS HOPE!
THAT'S WHY I ***NEVER*** GIVE UP!

TOWARDS THE ISLAND

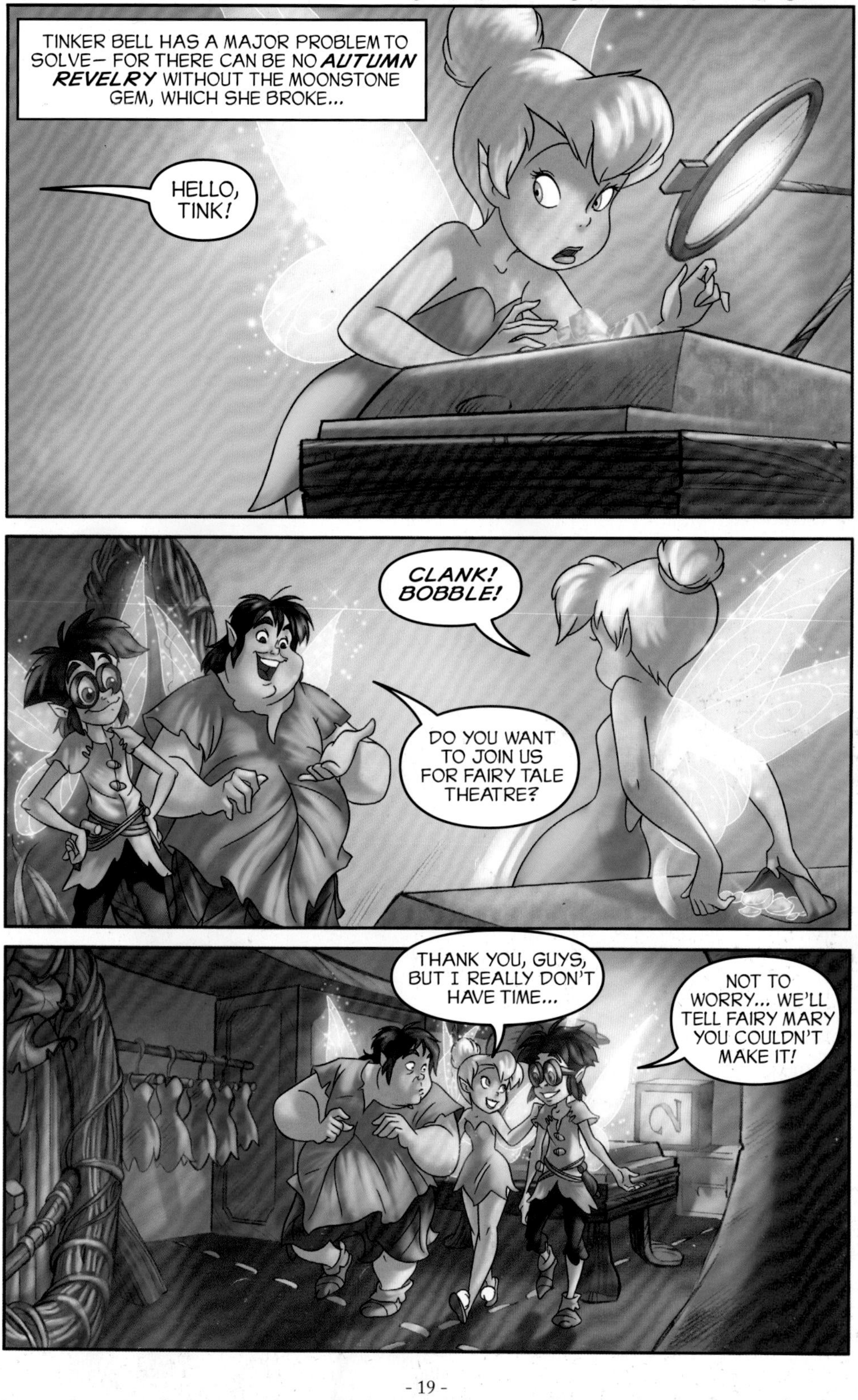

TINKER BELL HAS A MAJOR PROBLEM TO SOLVE– FOR THERE CAN BE NO *AUTUMN REVELRY* WITHOUT THE MOONSTONE GEM, WHICH SHE BROKE...
HELLO, TINK!
CLANK! BOBBLE!
DO YOU WANT TO JOIN US FOR FAIRY TALE THEATRE?
THANK YOU, GUYS, BUT I REALLY DON'T HAVE TIME...
NOT TO WORRY... WE'LL TELL FAIRY MARY YOU COULDN'T MAKE IT!

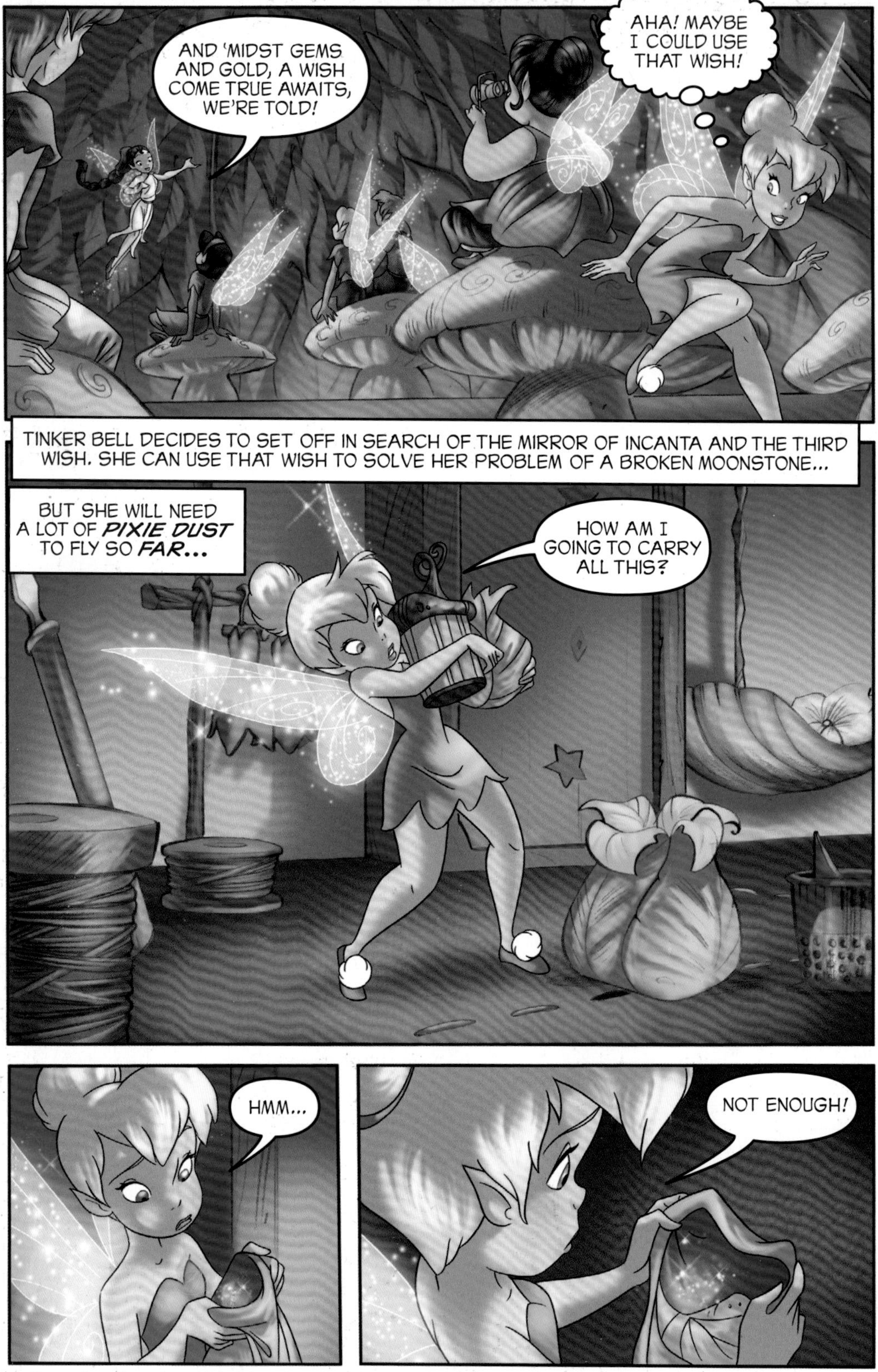
AND 'MIDST GEMS AND GOLD, A WISH COME TRUE AWAITS, WE'RE TOLD!
AHA! MAYBE I COULD USE THAT WISH!
TINKER BELL DECIDES TO SET OFF IN SEARCH OF THE MIRROR OF INCANTA AND THE THIRD WISH. SHE CAN USE THAT WISH TO SOLVE HER PROBLEM OF A BROKEN MOONSTONE...
BUT SHE WILL NEED A LOT OF PIXIE DUST TO FLY SO FAR...
HOW AM I GOING TO CARRY ALL THIS?
HMM...
NOT ENOUGH!

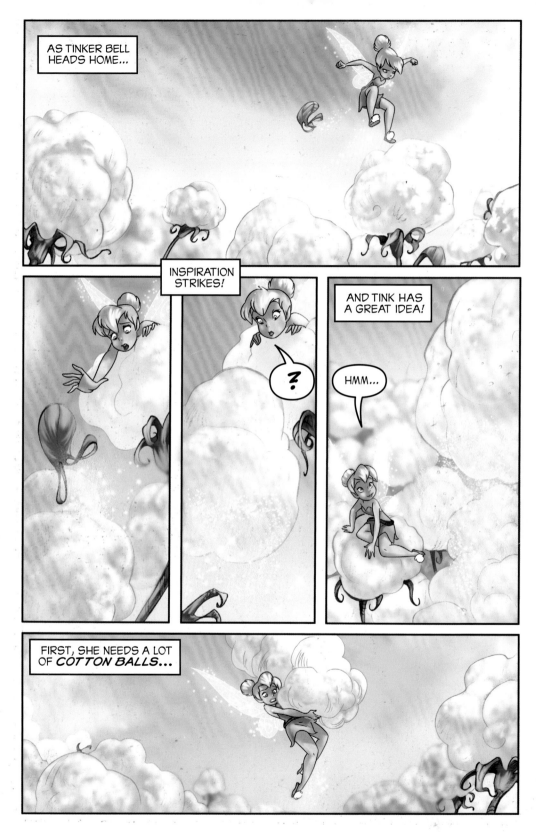

AS TINKER BELL HEADS HOME...

INSPIRATION STRIKES!

?

AND TINK HAS A GREAT IDEA!

HMM...

FIRST, SHE NEEDS A LOT OF *COTTON BALLS*...

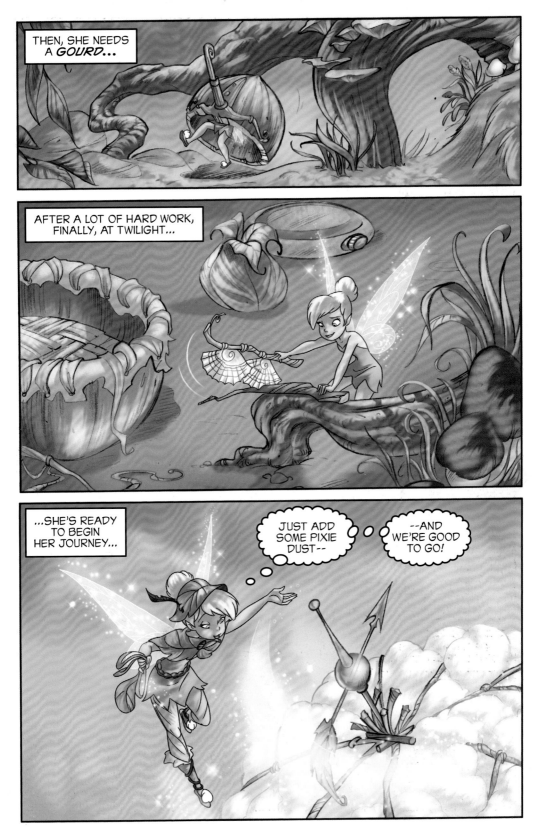

THEN, SHE NEEDS A *GOURD*...

AFTER A LOT OF HARD WORK, FINALLY, AT TWILIGHT...

...SHE'S READY TO BEGIN HER JOURNEY...

JUST ADD SOME PIXIE DUST--

--AND WE'RE GOOD TO GO!

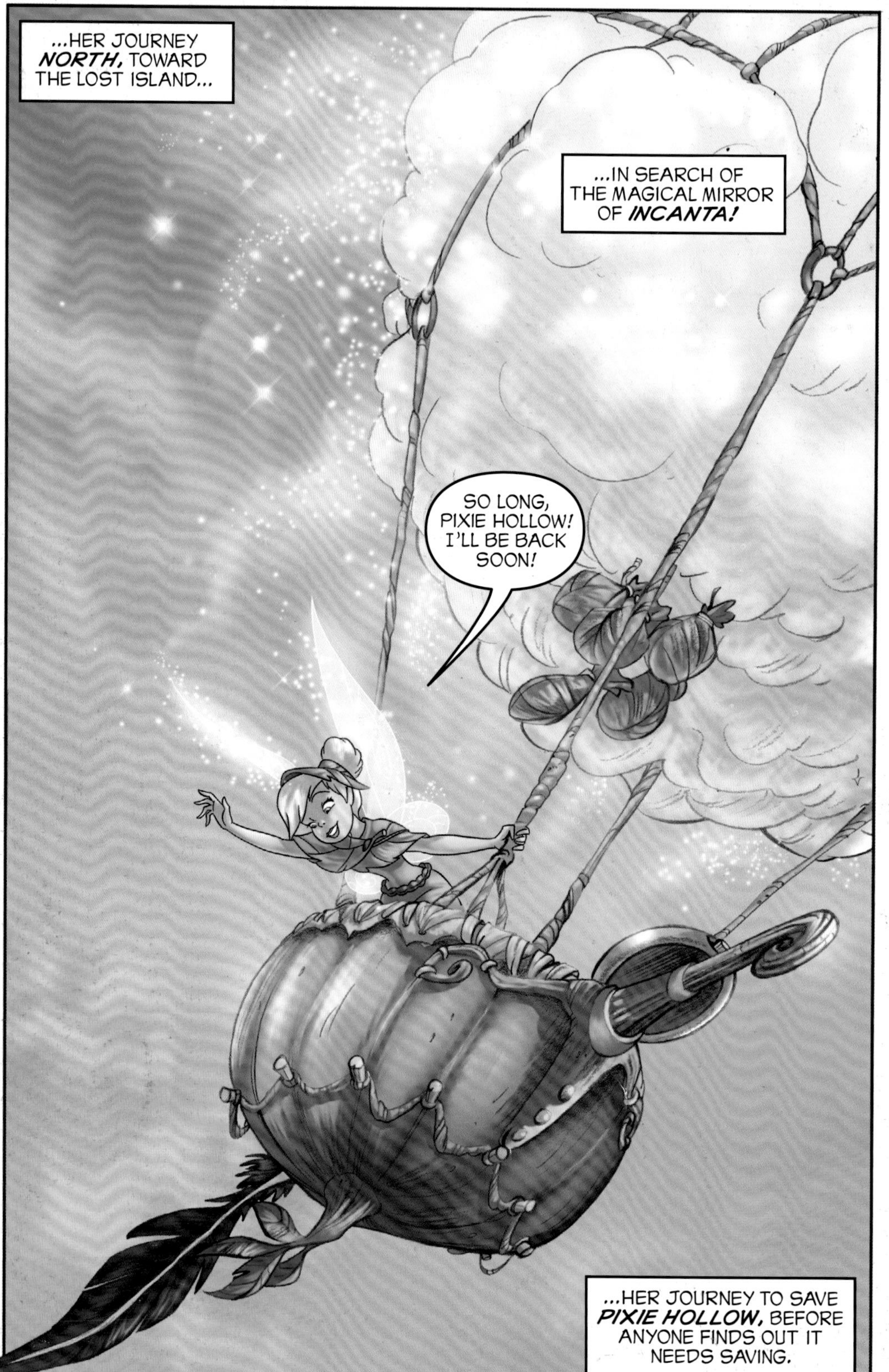
...HER JOURNEY NORTH, TOWARD THE LOST ISLAND...
...IN SEARCH OF THE MAGICAL MIRROR OF INCANTA!
SO LONG, PIXIE HOLLOW! I'LL BE BACK SOON!
...HER JOURNEY TO SAVE PIXIE HOLLOW, BEFORE ANYONE FINDS OUT IT NEEDS SAVING.

THE MAGICAL MIRROR OF INCANTA

TINKER BELL RACES THROUGH THE SKY, IN A FLYING SHIP SHE CREATED, ON A VERY IMPORTANT MISSION...

THE *AUTUMN REVELRY* IS COMING CLOSER AND CLOSER, WHICH IS WHEN THE RAYS OF A BLUE MOON SHINE THROUGH THE MOONSTONE, GENERATING THE PRECIOUS BLUE PIXIE DUST NEEDED TO REPLENISH THE PIXIE DUST TREE...

TINKER BELL WAS CHOSEN TO BUILD THE *AUTUMN SCEPTER* THAT HOLDS THE *MOONSTONE* DURING THE *AUTUMN REVELRY* BUT SHE ACCIDENTALLY *BROKE* BOTH THE SCEPTER AND THE MOONSTONE-- THE ONLY MOONSTONE THAT HAS BEEN FOUND IN THE LAST 100 YEARS!

SO NOW SHE'S LOOKING FOR THE MAGICAL MIRROR OF INCANTA, THAT CAN GRANT HER ONE VERY IMPORTANT WISH!

>WHEW!< ... I'M STARVING!

BUT... WHERE ARE MY BOYSENBERRY ROLLS?

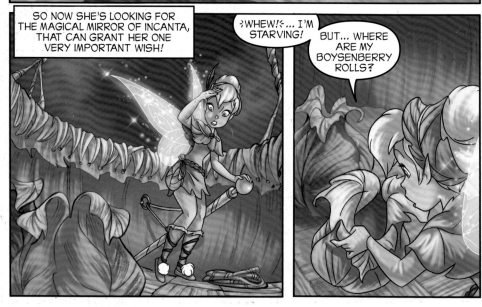

- 33 -

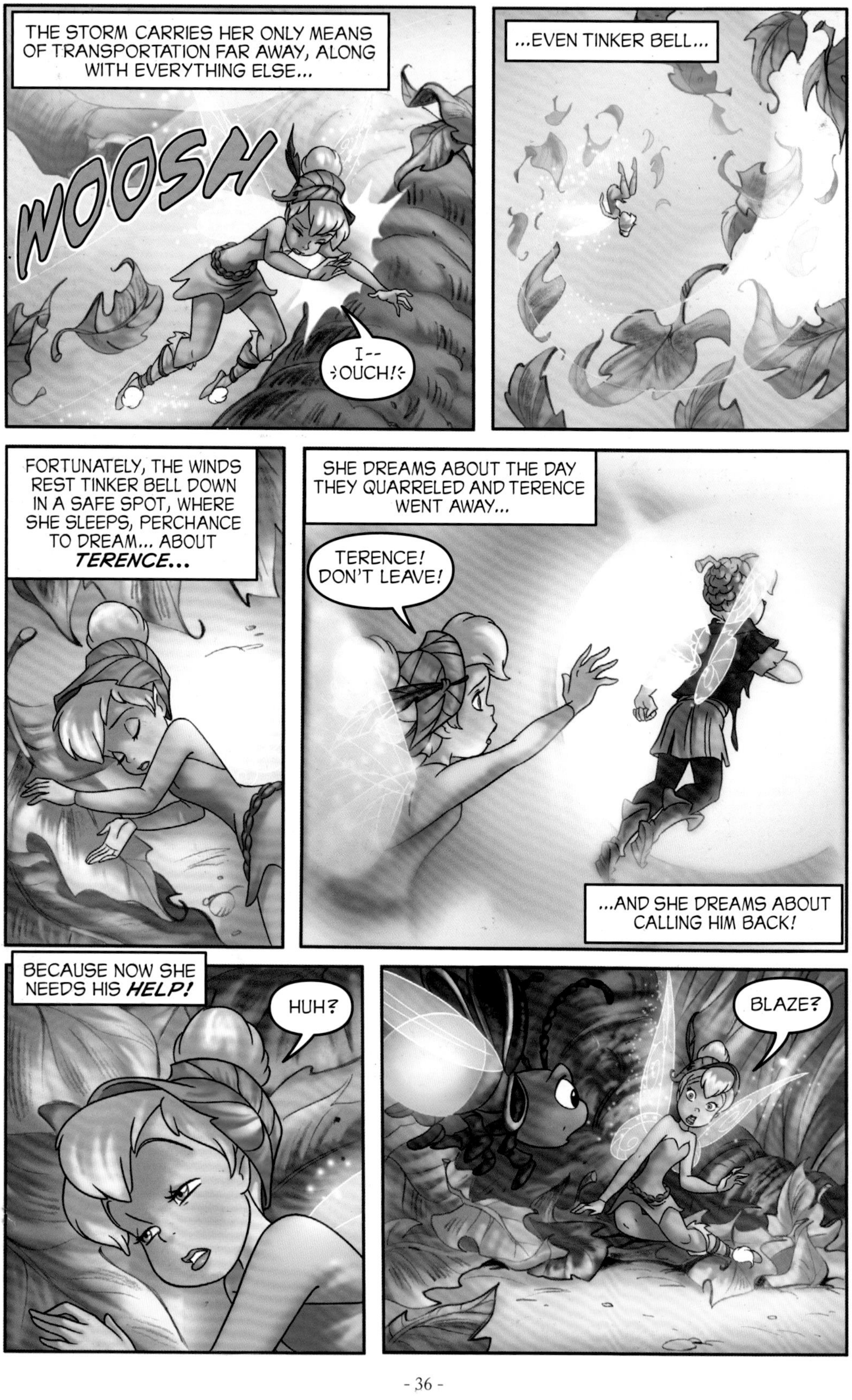
THE STORM CARRIES HER ONLY MEANS OF TRANSPORTATION FAR AWAY, ALONG WITH EVERYTHING ELSE...
WOOSH
I-- OUCH!
...EVEN TINKER BELL...
FORTUNATELY, THE WINDS REST TINKER BELL DOWN IN A SAFE SPOT, WHERE SHE SLEEPS, PERCHANCE TO DREAM... ABOUT *TERENCE...*
SHE DREAMS ABOUT THE DAY THEY QUARRELED AND TERENCE WENT AWAY...
TERENCE! DON'T LEAVE!
...AND SHE DREAMS ABOUT CALLING HIM BACK!
BECAUSE NOW SHE NEEDS HIS *HELP!*
HUH?
BLAZE?

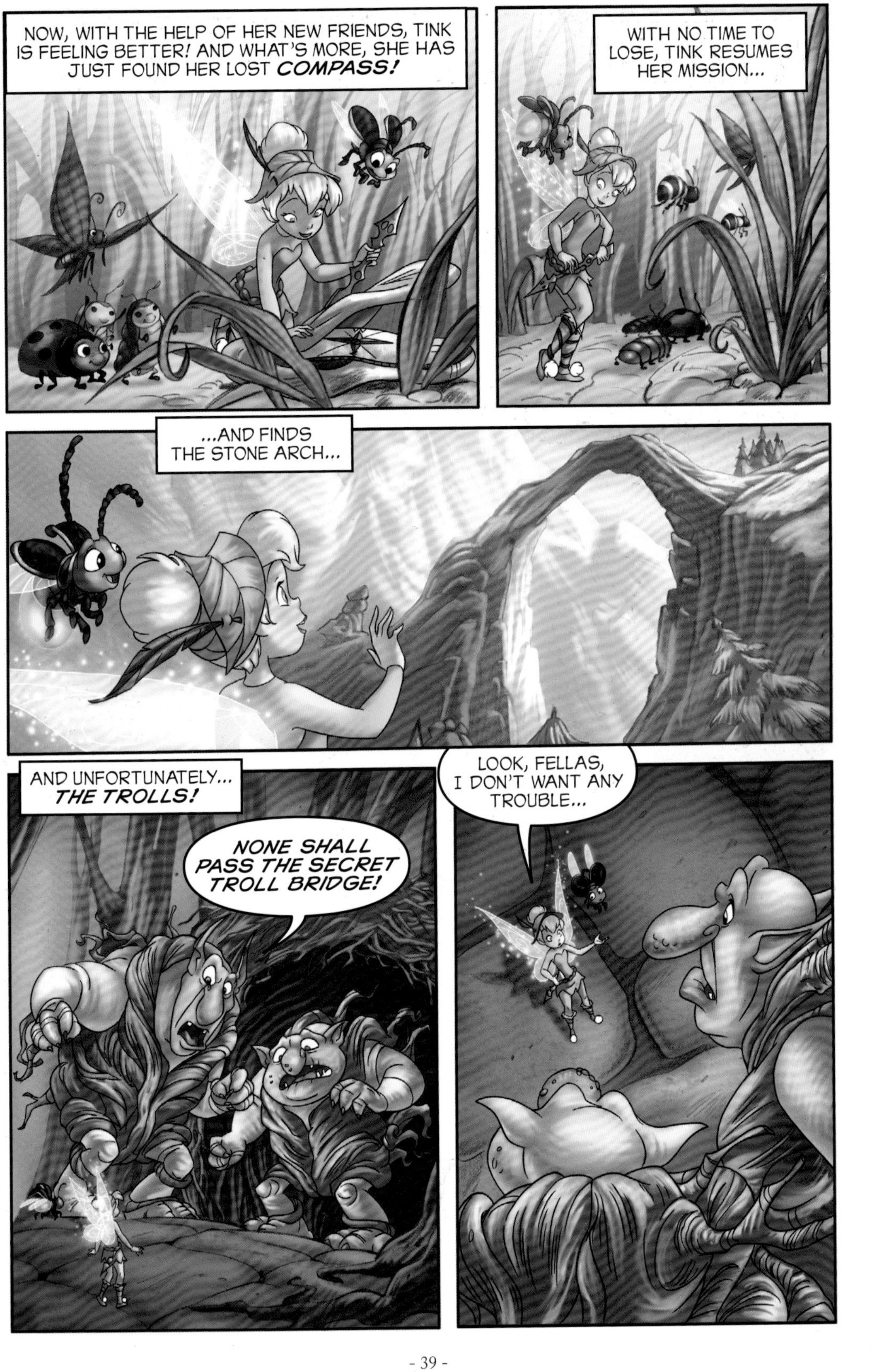
NOW, WITH THE HELP OF HER NEW FRIENDS, TINK IS FEELING BETTER! AND WHAT'S MORE, SHE HAS JUST FOUND HER LOST COMPASS!
WITH NO TIME TO LOSE, TINK RESUMES HER MISSION...
...AND FINDS THE STONE ARCH...
AND UNFORTUNATELY... THE TROLLS!
NONE SHALL PASS THE SECRET TROLL BRIDGE!
LOOK, FELLAS, I DON'T WANT ANY TROUBLE...

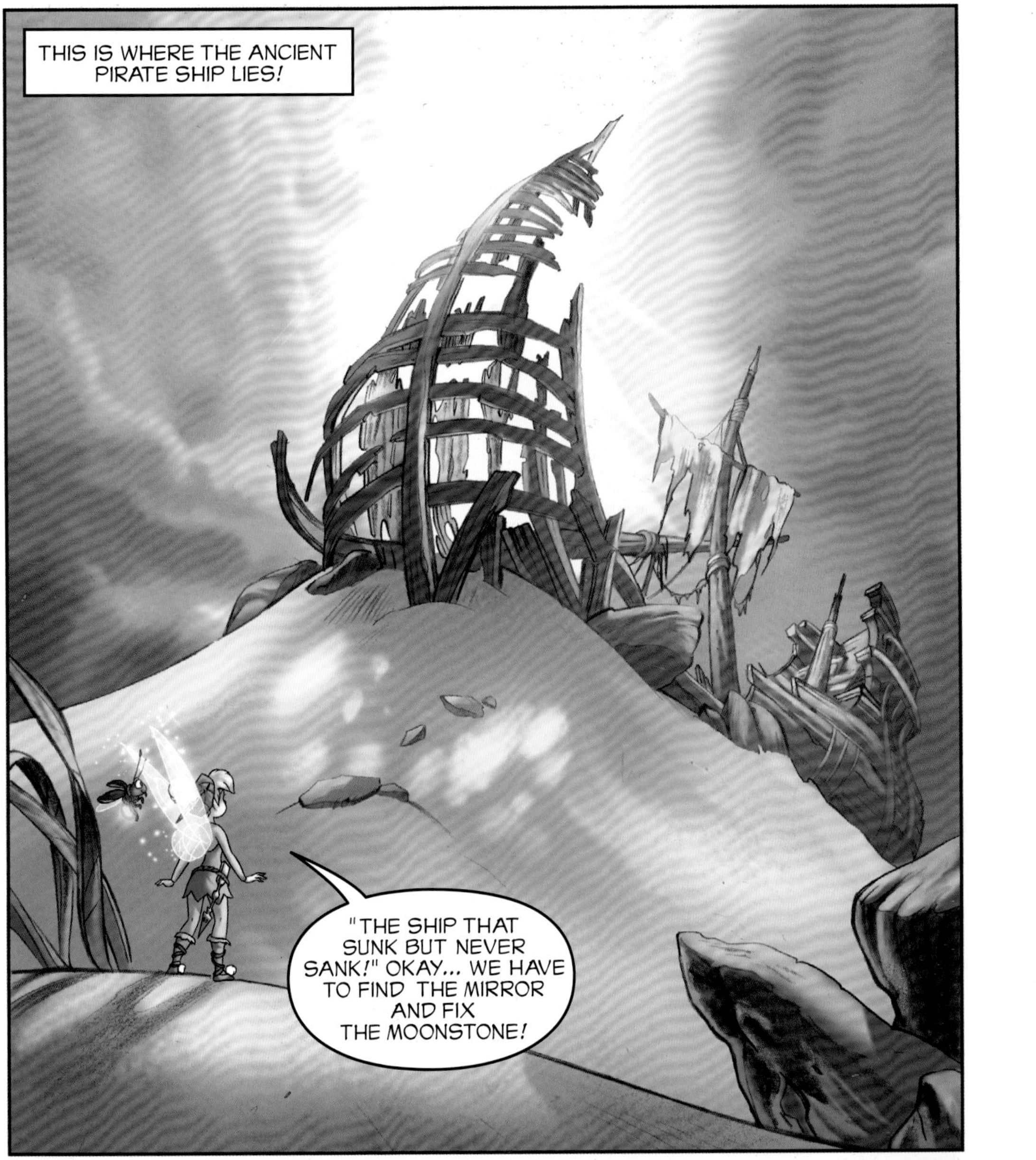
THIS IS WHERE THE ANCIENT PIRATE SHIP LIES!
"THE SHIP THAT SUNK BUT NEVER SANK!" OKAY... WE HAVE TO FIND THE MIRROR AND FIX THE MOONSTONE!

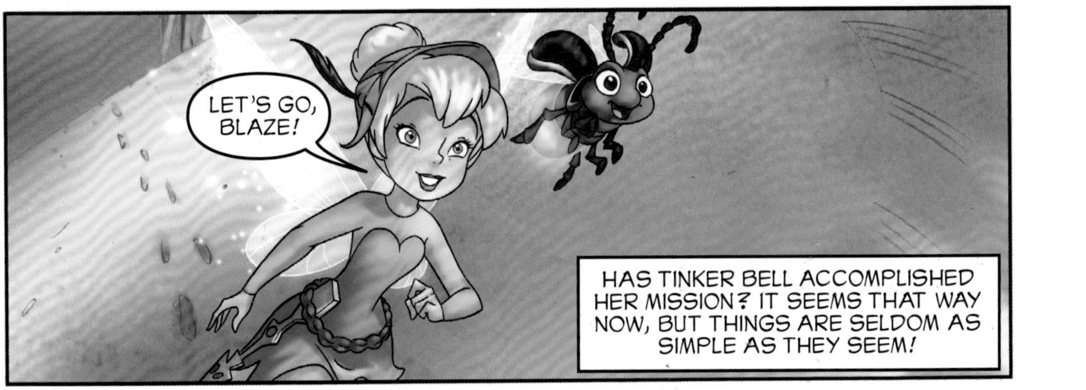
LET'S GO, BLAZE!
HAS TINKER BELL ACCOMPLISHED HER MISSION? IT SEEMS THAT WAY NOW, BUT THINGS ARE SELDOM AS SIMPLE AS THEY SEEM!

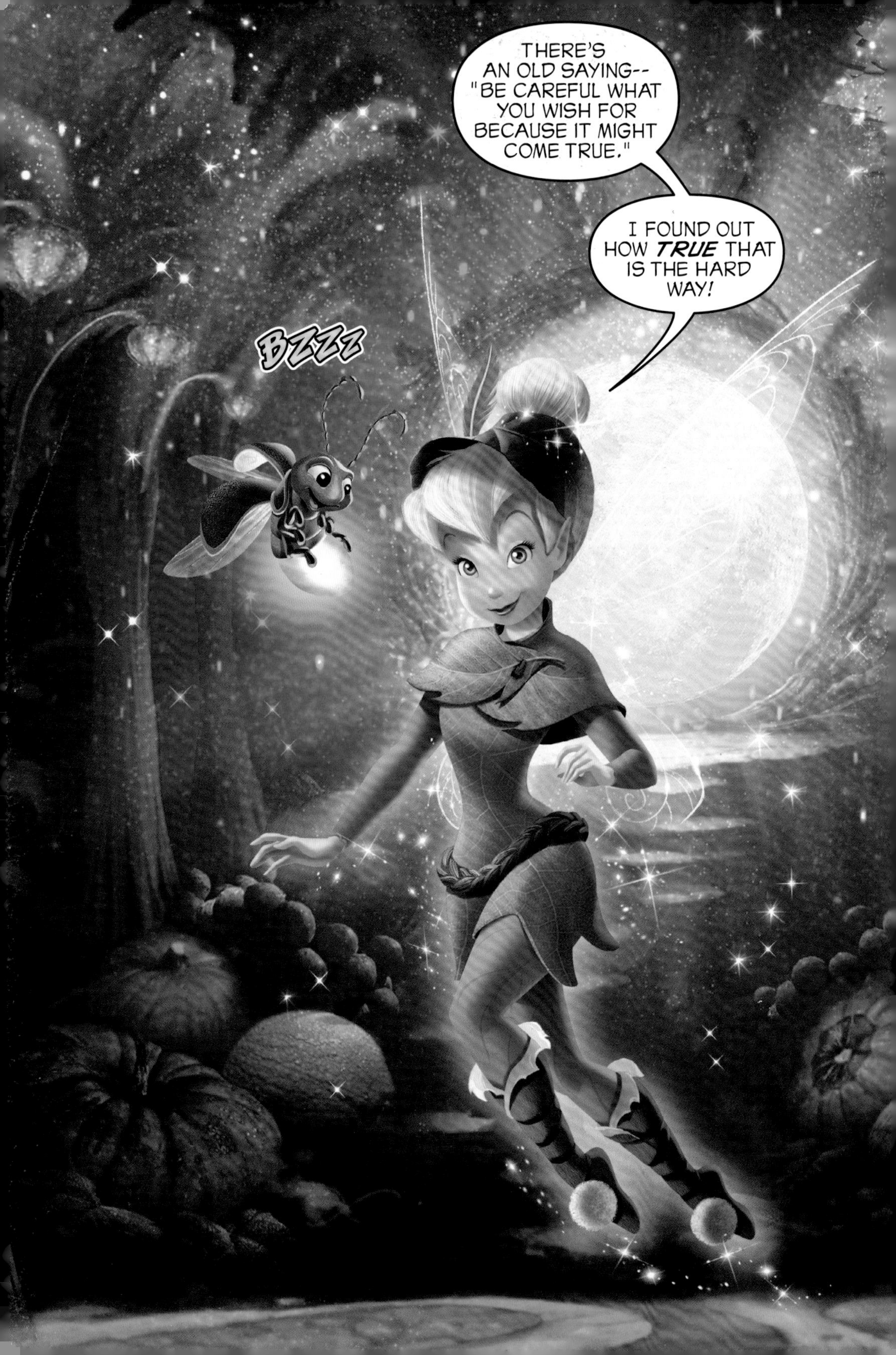
THERE'S AN OLD SAYING-- "BE CAREFUL WHAT YOU WISH FOR BECAUSE IT MIGHT COME TRUE."
I FOUND OUT HOW *TRUE* THAT IS THE HARD WAY!
BZZZ

THE GLOW OF FRIENDSHIP

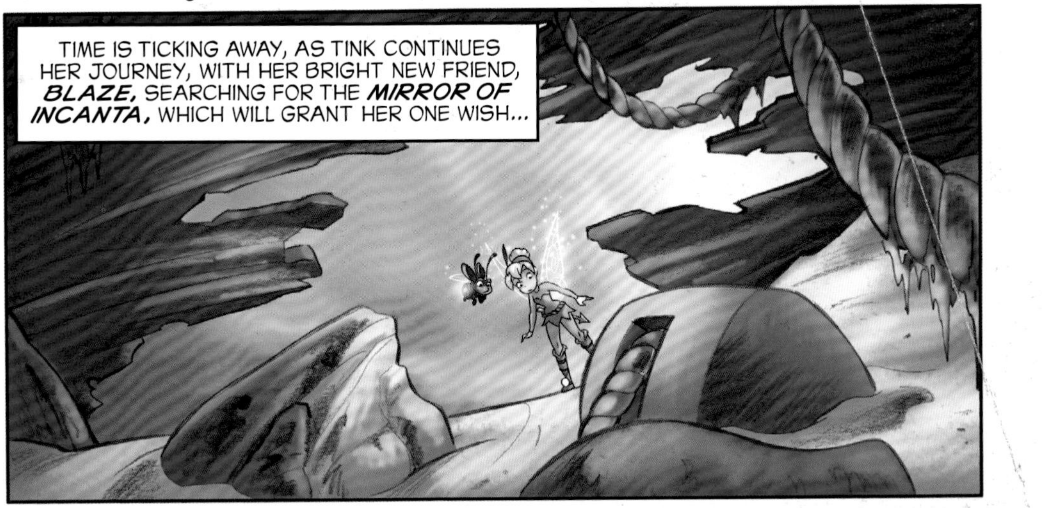
TIME IS TICKING AWAY, AS TINK CONTINUES HER JOURNEY, WITH HER BRIGHT NEW FRIEND, ***BLAZE,*** SEARCHING FOR THE ***MIRROR OF INCANTA,*** WHICH WILL GRANT HER ONE WISH...

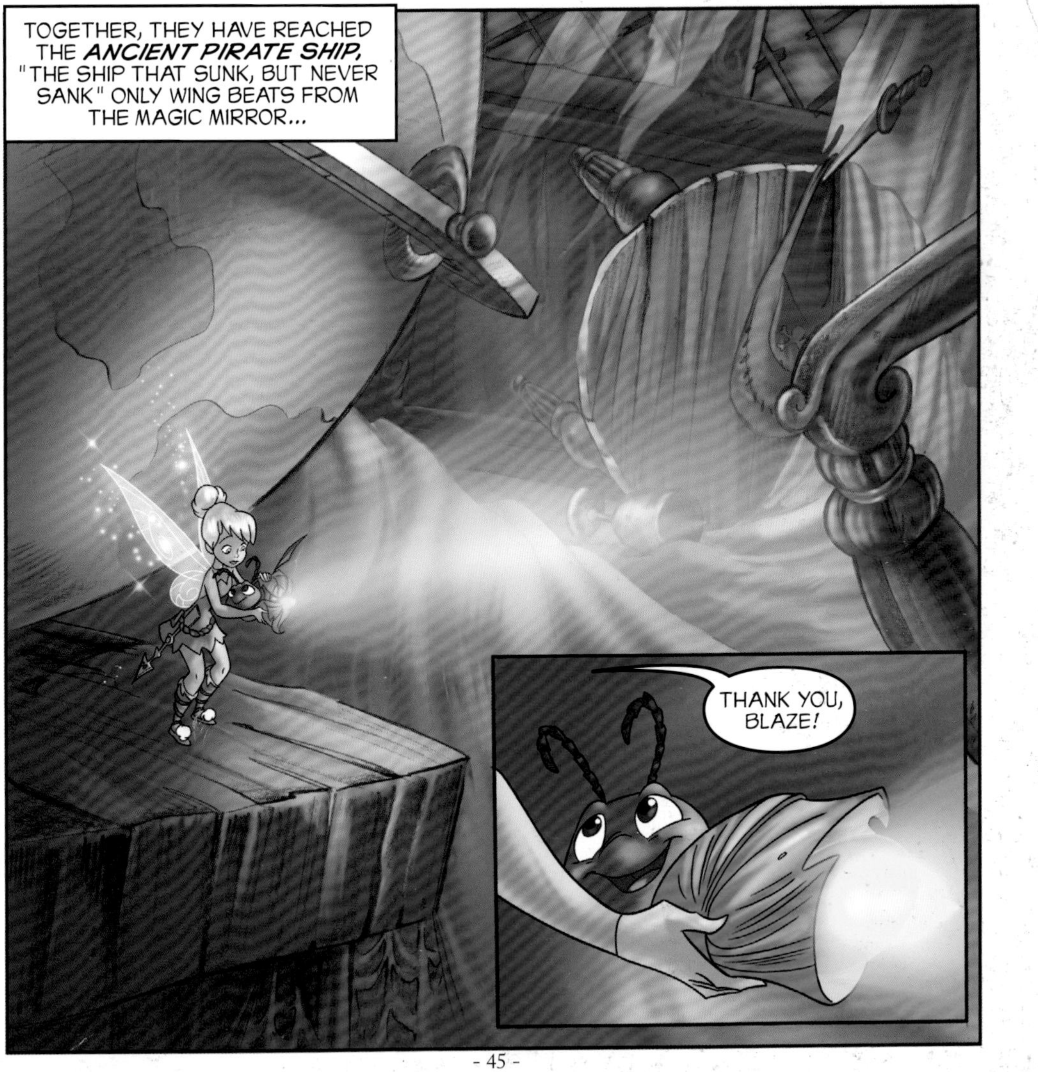
TOGETHER, THEY HAVE REACHED THE ***ANCIENT PIRATE SHIP,*** "THE SHIP THAT SUNK, BUT NEVER SANK" ONLY WING BEATS FROM THE MAGIC MIRROR...
THANK YOU, BLAZE!

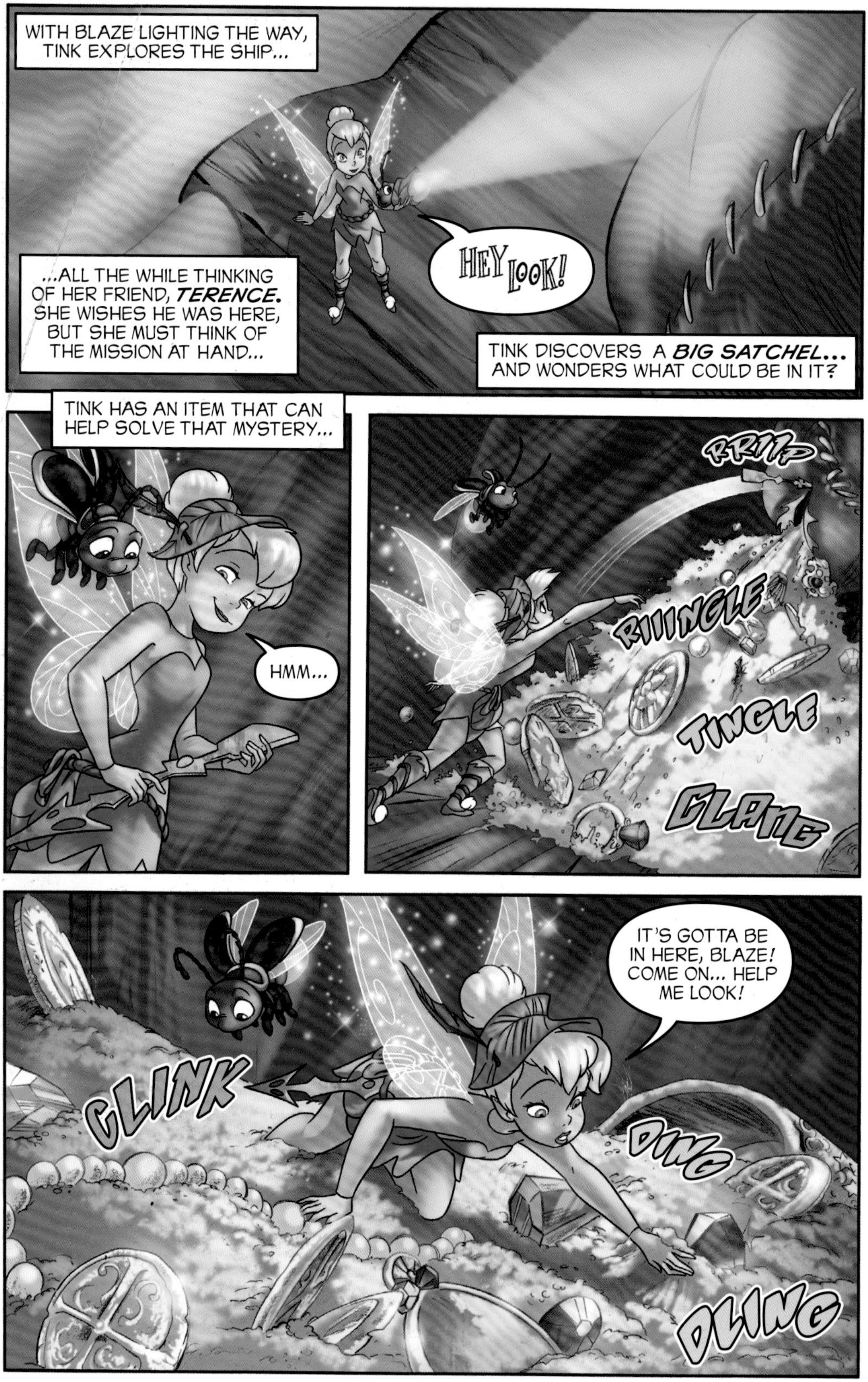
WITH BLAZE LIGHTING THE WAY, TINK EXPLORES THE SHIP...
HEY LOOK!
...ALL THE WHILE THINKING OF HER FRIEND, TERENCE. SHE WISHES HE WAS HERE, BUT SHE MUST THINK OF THE MISSION AT HAND...
TINK DISCOVERS A BIG SATCHEL... AND WONDERS WHAT COULD BE IN IT?
TINK HAS AN ITEM THAT CAN HELP SOLVE THAT MYSTERY...
HMM...
RRRIP
RIIINGLE
TINGLE
CLANG
IT'S GOTTA BE IN HERE, BLAZE! COME ON... HELP ME LOOK!
CLINK
DING
DLING

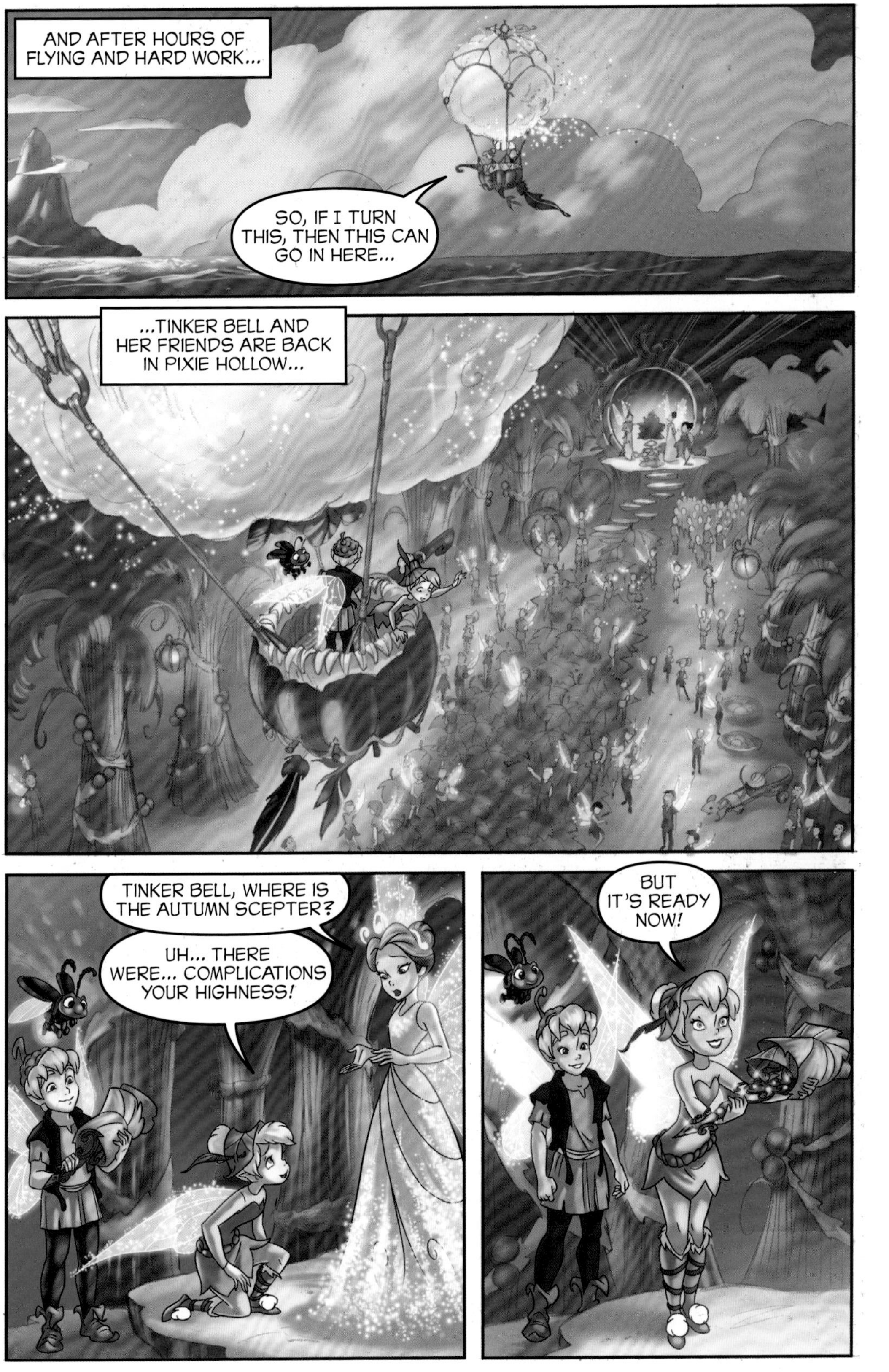
AND AFTER HOURS OF FLYING AND HARD WORK...
SO, IF I TURN THIS, THEN THIS CAN GO IN HERE...
...TINKER BELL AND HER FRIENDS ARE BACK IN PIXIE HOLLOW...
TINKER BELL, WHERE IS THE AUTUMN SCEPTER?
UH... THERE WERE... COMPLICATIONS YOUR HIGHNESS!
BUT IT'S READY NOW!

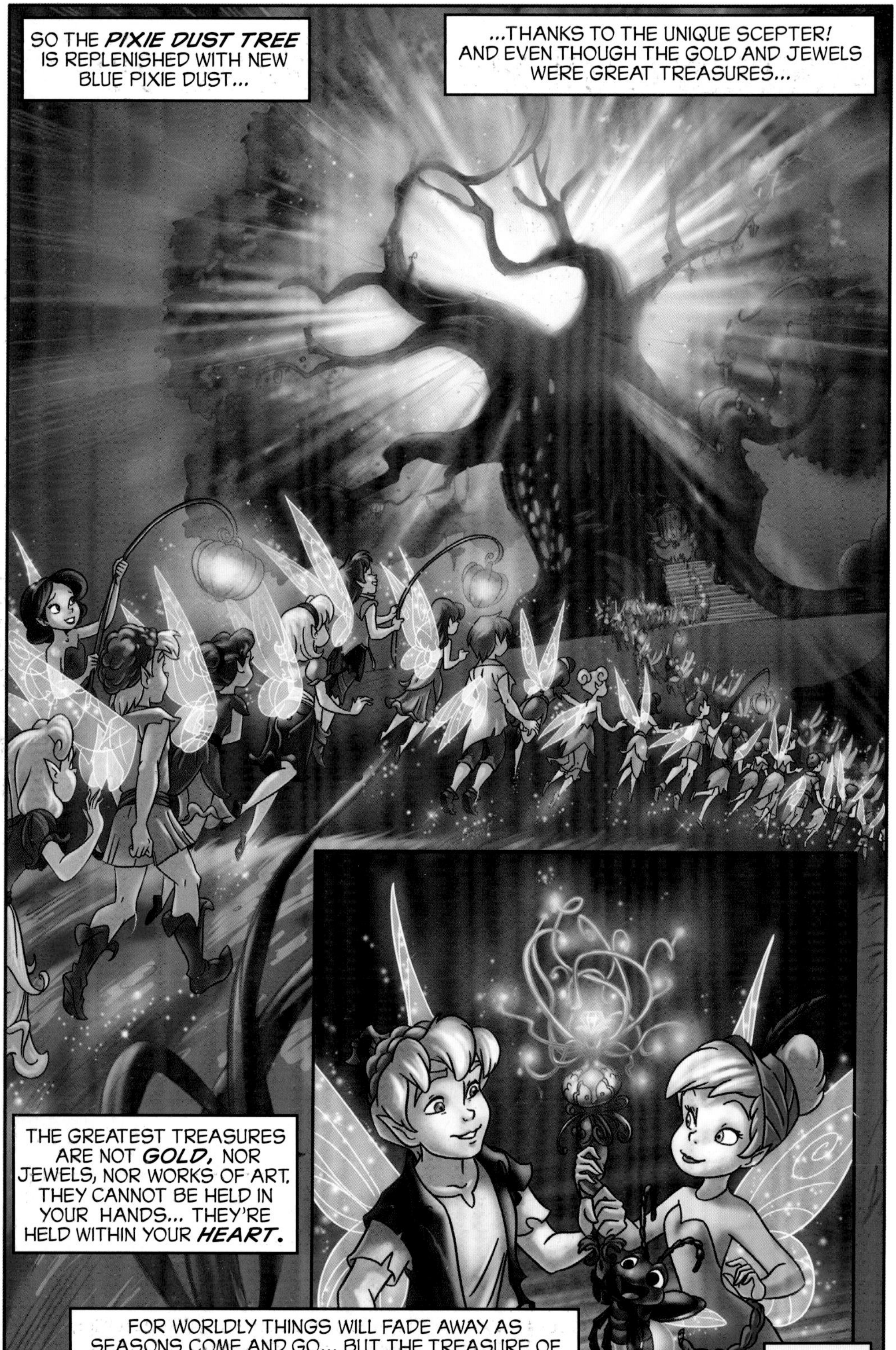
SO THE PIXIE DUST TREE IS REPLENISHED WITH NEW BLUE PIXIE DUST...
...THANKS TO THE UNIQUE SCEPTER! AND EVEN THOUGH THE GOLD AND JEWELS WERE GREAT TREASURES...
THE GREATEST TREASURES ARE NOT GOLD, NOR JEWELS, NOR WORKS OF ART. THEY CANNOT BE HELD IN YOUR HANDS... THEY'RE HELD WITHIN YOUR HEART.
FOR WORLDLY THINGS WILL FADE AWAY AS SEASONS COME AND GO... BUT THE TREASURE OF TRUE FRIENDSHIP WILL NEVER LOSE ITS GLOW.
THE END

WATCH OUT FOR PAPERCUTZ™

Welcome to the twelfth treasure-filled DISNEY FAIRIES graphic novel from Papercutz, those kids who refuse to ever grow up, dedicated to publishing great graphic novels for all ages! I'm Jim Salicrup, the Editor-in-Chief and professional Pixie Dust distributor.

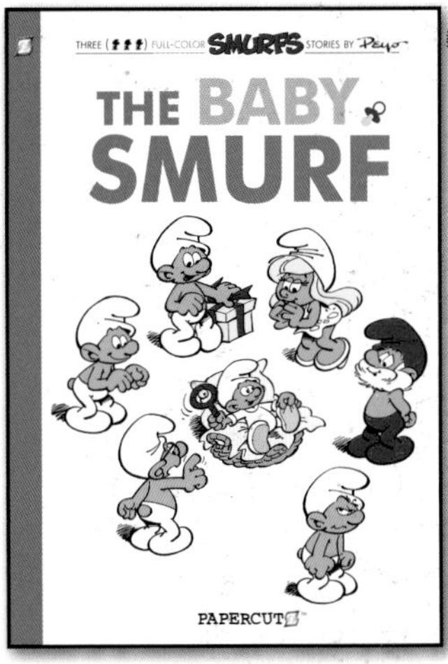
THREE FULL-COLOR SMURFS STORIES BY Peyo
THE BABY SMURF
PAPERCUTZ

Recently, I attended the birthday party for Cortney Faye Powell, who contributes revised dialogue and captions to DISNEY FAIRIES, and thought I'd share this pic of the lovely coconut birthday cake baked by her mom, the multi-talented Paulette Powell.

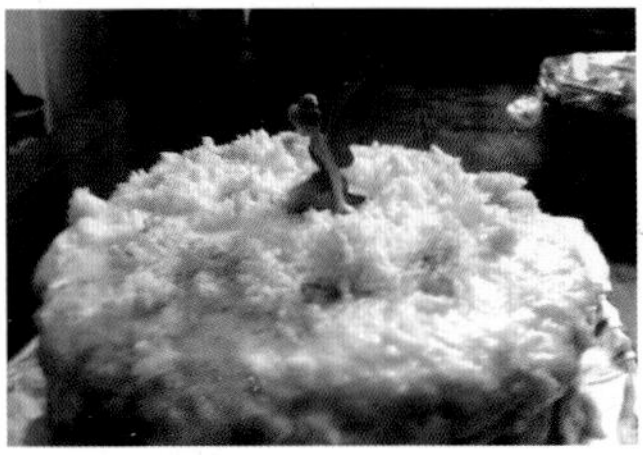

And, yes, it tasted as good as it looks!

In "The Scepter," there's a lot of talk about the Blue Moon! We learn that when the rays of the Blue Moon pass through the moonstone it creates Blue Pixie Dust that restores the Pixie Dust Tree! But it seems that's not all that happens when there's a full moon! According to Papa Smurf, "when the moon's blue, sometimes an extraordinary event can smurf, like for example, the coming of Baby Smurf!" For the full story, look for THE SMURFS #14 "The Baby Smurf," also from Papercutz.

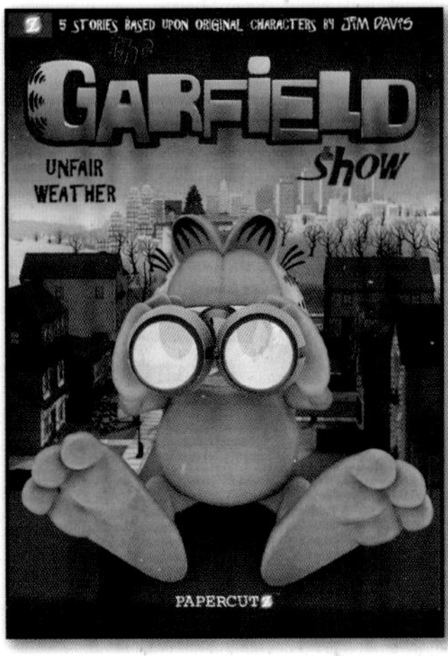
5 STORIES BASED UPON ORIGINAL CHARACTERS BY JIM DAVIS
The GARFIELD Show
UNFAIR WEATHER
PAPERCUTZ

In "The Glow of Friendship," Tinker Bell gets the opportunity to make a wish. Too bad she didn't wish for the Genie from Aladdin-- then she would've had a lot of wishes! In THE GARFIELD SHOW #1 "Unfair Weather," Garfield's friend Odie finds a genie in a bottle on the beach. Garfield thinks he has it all figured out, when he thinks, "I know exactly what my first wish would be. I would wish for a million more wishes. And just before I use all of them up, I'd wish for another million and then another, and then another..." Me? I just wish you'll come back and enjoy DISNEY FAIRIES #13 "Tinker Bell and the Pixie Hollow Games." Check out the special preview in a couple of pages. What do you wish for? Whatever it is, remember to keep believing in "faith, trust, and Pixie Dust"! It can't hurt!

Thanks,

Jim

STAY IN TOUCH!

EMAIL:	salicrup@papercutz.com
WEB:	www.papercutz.com
TWITTER:	@papercutzgn
FACEBOOK:	PAPERCUTZGRAPHICNOVELS
REGULAR MAIL:	Papercutz, 160 Broadway, Suite 700, East Wing, New York, NY 10038

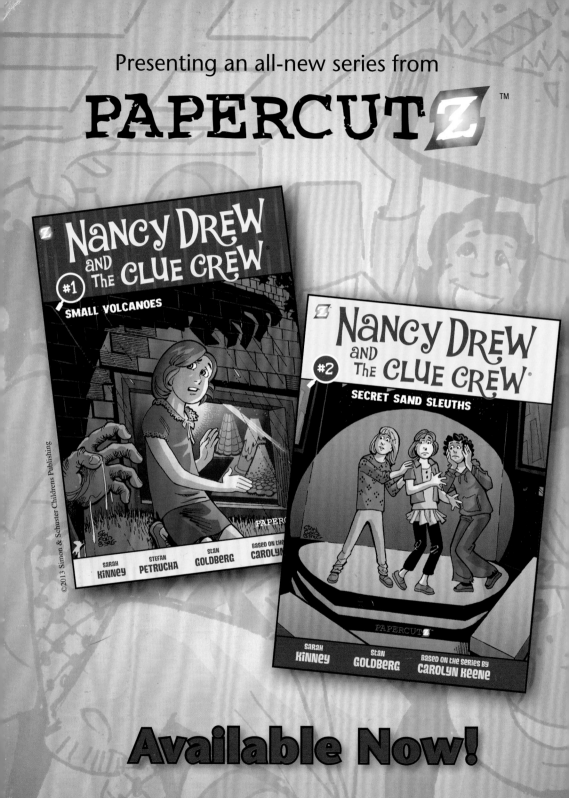

THE GARDEN FAIRIES HAVE NEVER WON THE *PIXIE HOLLOW GAMES* AND ROSETTA HAS NEVER TAKEN PART IN THEM, BUT THIS TIME THERE'S NO TURNING BACK: THE BIG DAY HAS ARRIVED!

BOBBLE WELCOMES THE FAIRY FANS AND INTRODUCES THE RULES!

THE GAMES WILL SPAN THE NEXT *THREE DAYS* WITH THE LAST-PLACE TEAM ELIMINATED AFTER EACH EVENT...

ALL LEADING UP TO THE PIXIE CART *DERBY*, WHERE THE FINAL FOUR TEAMS WILL RACE FOR THE CHAMPIONSHIP!

AND SO, LET THE GAMES--

LET THE GAMES BEGIN!

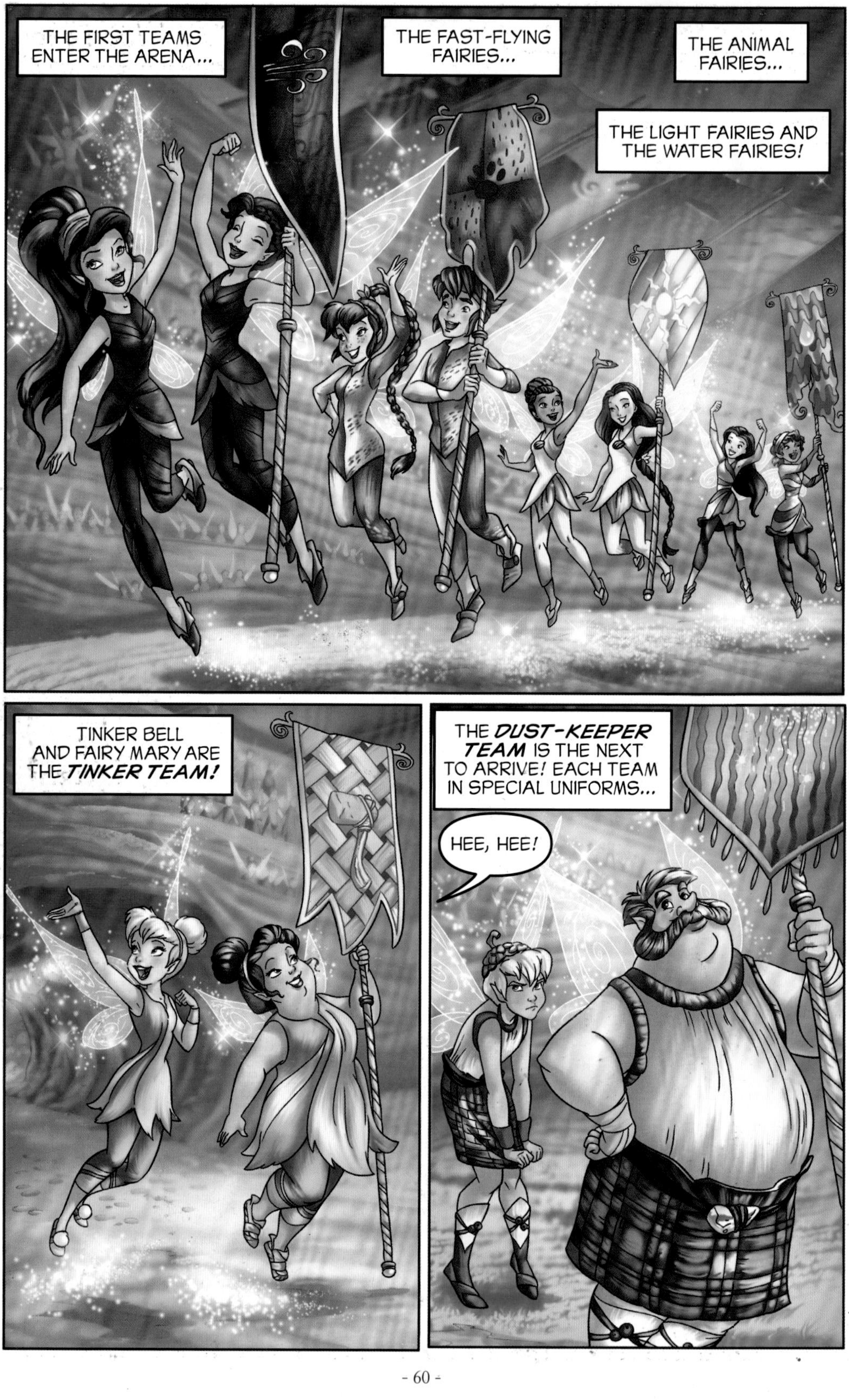
THE FIRST TEAMS ENTER THE ARENA...
THE FAST-FLYING FAIRIES...
THE ANIMAL FAIRIES...
THE LIGHT FAIRIES AND THE WATER FAIRIES!
TINKER BELL AND FAIRY MARY ARE THE *TINKER TEAM!*
THE *DUST-KEEPER TEAM* IS THE NEXT TO ARRIVE! EACH TEAM IN SPECIAL UNIFORMS...
HEE, HEE!

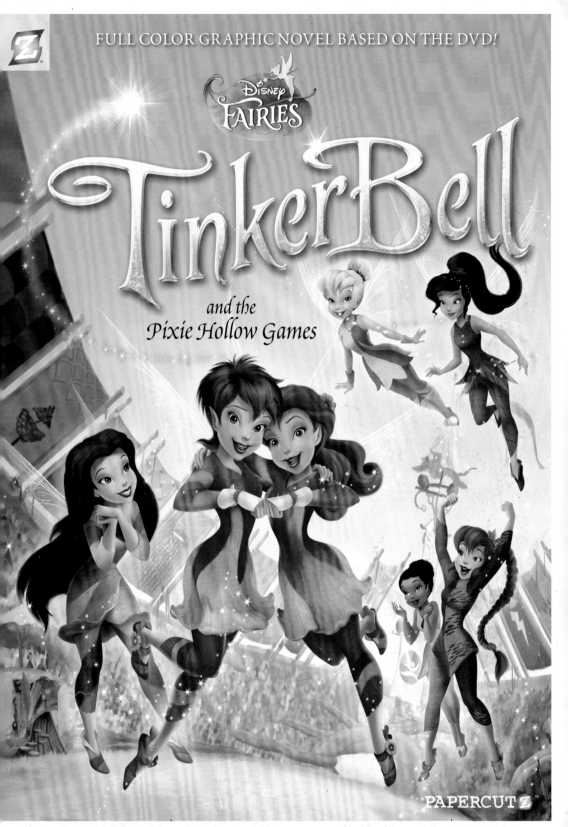

FULL COLOR GRAPHIC NOVEL BASED ON THE DVD!

DISNEY FAIRIES

Tinker Bell

and the
Pixie Hollow Games

PAPERCUTZ

Don't miss DISNEY FAIRIES #13 "Tinker Bell and the Pixie Hollow Games"!

More Great Graphic Novels from PAPERCUTZ™

THEA STILTON #2
"Revenge of the Lizard Club"
Meet the Thea Sisters of
Mouseford Academy!

ERNEST & REBECCA #4
"The Land of Walking Stones"
A 6 ½ year old girl and her
microbial buddy against the world!

SYBIL THE BACKPACK FAIRY #4
"Princes Nina"
Sybil and Nina's excellent adventure
through time!

GERONIMO STILTON #13
"The Fastest Train in the West"
Geronimo Stilton... cowboy?

THE SMURFS #15
"The Smurflings"
Why are the Smurfs getting
younger?

ARiOL #2
"Thunder Horse"
Meet ARiOL, a donkey just
like you and me, trying to
survive life at school.